"I want to be v

Raoul's meaning was unmistakable.

"Are you suggesting we scratch an *itch?*" Stephanie demanded.

Her scandalized expression amused him. "When I take you to bed," he vowed silkily, "it won't be merely to *scratch an itch!*"

"No," Stephanie denied heatedly. "Because you won't get anywhere near my bed!"

Raoul regarded her silently for a few seconds. "You are so sure about that?"

HELEN BIANCHIN was born in New Zealand and traveled to Australia before marrying her Italian-born husband. After three years they moved, returned to New Zealand with their daughter, had two sons then resettled in Australia. Encouraged by friends to recount anecdotes of her years as a tobacco sharefarmer's wife living in an Italian community, Helen began setting words on paper, and her first novel was published in 1975. An animal lover, she says her terrier and new Persian kitten consider her study to be as much theirs as hers.

USA Today bestselling author **Helen Bianchin** loves to create sizzling emotional tension, passion and conflict between her characters—especially when it leads to marriage!

In *The Marriage Deal* (Presents #2097), Michel Lanier discovered that sparks continue to fly even *after* the wedding! Now it's his brother's turn. Raoul Lanier is equally gorgeous and passionate—and he's about to meet his match in Stephanie!

Helen Bianchin

THE HUSBAND ASSIGNMENT

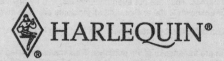

HARLEQUIN®

TORONTO • NEW YORK • LONDON
AMSTERDAM • PARIS • SYDNEY • HAMBURG
STOCKHOLM • ATHENS • TOKYO • MILAN • MADRID
PRAGUE • WARSAW • BUDAPEST • AUCKLAND

ISBN 0-373-12115-6

THE HUSBAND ASSIGNMENT

First North American Publication 2000.

Visit us at www.eHarlequin.com

Printed in U.S.A.

CHAPTER ONE

RAOUL LANIER inclined his head in silent acknowledgment as the attractive airline hostess extended a customary farewell to passengers leaving the aircraft.

Her mouth curved a little wider, and the expression in her eyes offered numerous sensual delights should he choose to extend an invitation to share a drink during her stopover.

The attention she'd bestowed on him during the long international flight had included a friendly warmth that went beyond the courteous solicitousness proffered to his fellow travelers.

It could have proved an interesting diversion, if fleeting sexual encounters formed part of his personal agenda, Raoul mused as he cleared the aircraft and entered the concourse.

As the eldest son and part heir to a billion-dollar fortune, a sense of caution coupled with cynicism had formed at an early age.

Good European genes had blessed him with enviable height, superb bone structure and ruggedly attractive facial features that inevitably drew a second glance. Physical fitness and fine clothes completed a combination that proved magnetic to women of all ages.

A quality that was both an advantage and a curse, he acknowledged with rueful humor as he rode the escalator down to ground level and crossed to the appropriate luggage carousel.

Raoul checked his watch. He had two hours in which to clear customs, take a cab to the hotel at Double Bay, shower and change, before he was scheduled to appear at a business meeting.

Primarily his Australian visit was intended to target the possibility of setting up a Sydney base for the multinational Lanier conglomerate. Wheels had already been set in motion, and if all the details met with his satisfaction, he was prepared to clinch the deal.

Not easily, for he was a skilled tactician whose strategy was recognized and lauded by his peers and associates.

He spotted his luggage, hefted it from the carousel and then strode out of the terminal to summon a taxi.

Brilliant summer sunshine had him reaching for protective sunglasses as he provided the driver with the name of his hotel, then he sank back against the seat in contemplative silence.

The meeting this afternoon held importance. He planned to present a noncommittal persona, and absent himself from the scene for several days, reachable only by cell phone during a sojourn on Queensland's Gold Coast.

Checking up on family. His mouth thinned slightly as his expression assumed reflective thought.

He held filial affection for both his brothers. The

youngest, Sebastian, had recently married and was at present taking an extended holiday in Europe with his new wife.

However, it was Michel who was providing concern, with his marriage of six months in apparent crisis. Seven weeks ago Michel's wife had left New York and flown to Australia to take part in a movie being filmed at the Gold Coast Warner Brothers' studios.

Michel had concluded important European meetings, then followed Sandrine with a view to negotiating a reconciliation. The fact the movie had developed financial problems merely added a bargaining dimension Raoul suspected Michel intended to use to his advantage.

Each of the Lanier brothers possessed a considerable personal fortune, and sinking a few million dollars into a floundering movie wouldn't put a dent in Michel's assets.

A sudden screech of brakes, a muffled curse from the taxi driver, followed by an offered apology captured his attention, and he caught the buildup of traffic, the terrace houses, as the driver swung into the outer lane.

Raoul caught a glimpse of tall buildings stretched skyward in the distance, and estimated it would take ten minutes, fifteen at most, to reach the Ritz-Carlton hotel in Double Bay.

He was no stranger to this large southern hemispheric city, and he held a certain affection for its scenic beauty and stunning architecture, albeit that it was very young in terms of his native France.

Home was a luxury two-story apartment in Auteuil filled with antique furniture, marble-tiled floors, oriental rugs, objets d'art.

He had been born and raised in Paris, graduated from one of its finest universities, then was absorbed into the Lanier corporation as a junior executive.

Raoul gave a grim smile in memory of those early days beneath his father's eaglelike tutelage. Henri Lanier had been a hard taskmaster. Ruthless, Raoul conceded, but fair.

Today, Henri presided as the figurehead of a multinational conglomerate, with Raoul and Michel holding equal power. Sebastian, on the other hand, had chosen law, graduated, practiced, then he penned and sold his first novel, and the rest as they say was history.

The taxi slid to a halt outside the entrance to a gracious well-established hotel a short distance from the waterfront.

Raoul handed the driver a folded note, then stepped from the vehicle while the concierge collected his bags from the boot.

Checking in was a simple procedure, and in his room he took bottled water from the bar-fridge and drank it, ordered room service to deliver lunch at midday, then he unpacked a few essentials, showered, shaved, donned a complimentary robe and replaced the receiver on the last of a few calls less than a minute before a steward presented lunch.

Afterward he dressed, checked his briefcase and took the lift to the main lobby. His meeting was scheduled for two. It was now three minutes past the hour. Essential minutes that gave him an edge, unless the man he was due to liaise with was also well-versed in tactical game-playing.

Eagerness inevitably bred punctuality, Raoul acknowledged, especially when the possibility of a large investment was at stake.

The meeting could easily have stretched to an hour. Raoul cut that time in half with clear instruction and assertive demand, leaving no shred of doubt as to who held command.

Afterward he returned to his room, snagged bottled water from the bar-fridge, then he opened his laptop and spent time keying in data and directing it via e-mail to Paris. He made two calls, the second of which was to Michel, alerting him to his arrival the following day.

Raoul flexed his limbs, then stretched his lengthy frame. He needed exercise. The gym? First, he'd exchange the business suit for sweats and sneakers, and take a walk in the fresh air. His plans for the evening encompassed nothing more than ordering in a light evening meal, followed by an hour or two on the laptop, then he intended to fall into bed and catch up on sleep.

The intercom buzzed, and Stephanie reached out to activate it.

'Michel Lanier is here.'

She winced at the receptionist's attempt at a French pronunciation, and stifled a faint smile at the girl's obvious effort to impress. Michel Lanier was, she had to concede, an impressive man. If a woman was susceptible to a tall, dark-haired, attractive male.

'Give me a minute, then show him in.'

It was an integral part of Stephanie's job as a marketing manager to initiate discussions and venture opinions. She liked what she did for a living, it paid well and the rewards were many.

There was satisfaction in utilizing her expertise in film, together with an instinctive grasp of what attracted and titillated public interest, thus improving cinema attendance, and profitability for the film studios, the investors.

This particular movie had gone over budget, over time, financial avenues had been exhausted and a week ago it had been destined not to be completed.

The crux had been Sandrine Lanier, part-time model and actress, who had a minor role in the film, and her husband's willingness to inject a considerable amount of money to salvage it.

Stephanie shuffled the papers she'd been perusing into a folder at the sound of a double knock on her door, and hit the Save button on her computer.

'Michel and Raoul Lanier.'

She successfully hid her surprise as she registered both names, and she stood and summoned a friendly smile as Michel Lanier entered the room.

'Please take a seat,' she instructed, indicating a pair of comfortable leather chairs.

'My brother requested he sit in at this meeting,' Michel Lanier revealed smoothly. 'You have no objection?'

What could she say? 'No, of course not.'

Michel made the introduction. 'Stephanie Sommers. Raoul Lanier.'

In his late thirties, she surmised, and the elder, if only by a few years.

Raoul Lanier stood an inch, maybe closer to two, taller than his brother. His broad frame held a familial similarity, as did his facial features. Except his hair was darker, almost black, and his jaw had the dark shadow of a man who was forced to shave night and morning.

Wide-set gray eyes, dark as slate, were far too knowledgeable for a woman's peace of mind. As to his mouth…its curve held a sensuality that hinted at great passion. Equally she imagined those lines could thin, perhaps become almost cruel if he was so inclined.

His presence in her office hinted *business,* which raised doubt in her mind that Michel Lanier held the sole stake in a financial package aimed at rescuing the film in which his wife played a minor part.

'Stephanie.' He extended his hand in formal greeting, and she took it, choosing to ignore the faint tinge of mockery evident.

His handshake was firm, his touch warm, and she told herself the sensual awareness pulsing through her veins was merely a figment of her imagination.

'Mr. Lanier,' she acknowledged coolly.

One eyebrow rose, and his mouth curved slightly. 'Raoul.' He lifted a hand and indicated Michel with an expressive gesture. 'Otherwise an adherence to formality will prove confusing.'

His accent was slight, but evident nonetheless, and the depth and intonation of his voice curled around her nerve endings and tugged a little, setting her internal protective mechanism on edge.

Charm, he had it. There was also knowledge apparent in those dark eyes, a knowledge that was wholly sensual, sexual, coupled with contemplative interest.

He would be lethal with women, she deduced wryly. Given his looks, his physique, his wealth, he wouldn't even have to try.

With deliberate movements, she crossed around her desk and sank into the leather chair. It was a position of power, and she used it mercilessly.

'I have the figures you requested.' She looked at Michel, and chose to ignore Raoul entirely. 'Together with a rundown of proposals we intend to use in promoting the film.' She picked up a manila envelope and slid papers into it. 'I'm sure you'll find it satisfactory. Of course, we can't begin with promotion until the film is completed. The marketing people will have a private viewing, then discuss which aspects should be highlighted to attract the attention of the viewing public.'

She kept her attention on Michel. 'I believe the producer anticipates another week should wrap up filming, with perhaps a further few days scheduled for reshooting. It would be of added interest to include you in the publicity campaign…both as an investor, and Sandrine's husband.' Her smile was purely professional. 'I trust you'll be agreeable?'

When he didn't respond, she explained, 'It's all part of the bid to protect your investment.' Did she sound cynical? She hadn't meant to, but it had been a long day. 'Do you have any questions?'

'You have another appointment?' Raoul queried silkily.

'Yes, I do.' Stephanie glanced at her watch, and stood. 'I'm sorry I can't spare you more time.' She met Michel's enigmatic gaze, then picked up the manila envelope and held it out to him. 'When you've examined these, please feel free to call me with any queries.'

'I'd like the opportunity to continue this discussion,' Raoul indicated. 'Shall we say dinner, tonight? Michel and Sandrine will join us. I'm staying at the Sheraton Mirage. Six-thirty in the main lobby?'

It annoyed her unreasonably that he took her acceptance for granted. 'I'm sorry, I won't be able to make it.'

'A date you can't break in the interest of business?'

Important business. Or was Raoul Lanier merely employing undue influence in his own interest?

'With my daughter, Mr. Lanier, whom I'm due to collect from the day care center in half an hour.' Her personal file was easily accessible to anyone with the right connections. Eliciting such details would be a breeze for someone of Michel or Raoul Lanier's standing.

His eyes narrowed fractionally. 'It isn't possible for you to hire a baby-sitter?'

She wanted to hit him for attempting to infringe on her personal life. 'Difficult, at such short notice,' she responded stiffly.

'Make the call, Stephanie.'

She disliked being controlled, and she resented this man's aura of power.

There was the temptation to tell him to go to hell, and she barely managed to bite her tongue. Michel Lanier was a wealthy man in his own right, although she couldn't be certain part of his investment wasn't being funded by the Lanier conglomerate. In which case, Raoul Lanier had a legitimate claim.

She could insist on another evening. In fact, she was sorely tempted to do just that. Except it seemed foolish to be irksome just for the sake of it.

Her expression was cool and composed as she inclined her head. 'If you'll excuse me?' She walked to the door and opened it, waiting as both men filed past her and exited the room.

One pair of dark gray eyes held a glimmer of amusement, and her own sharpened, then deepened with silent anger.

He was enjoying this, and didn't appear to give a second's consideration to what it would cost her in time and effort.

She closed the door behind them, then she crossed to her desk and pressed the required digits to connect with the teenage student she relied on to baby-sit. A few minutes later she replaced the receiver, gave a heavy sigh, then walked out to reception.

Michel Lanier was using his cell phone, and she was acutely conscious of Raoul's studied appraisal as she crossed to his side.

'Six-thirty, the Sheraton Mirage foyer,' she confirmed, adding with a certain cynicism, 'I shall look forward to it.'

He withdrew a slim billfold. 'My card, with my cell phone number.'

She wanted to ignore the courtesy, and add with cutting sarcasm that Hell could freeze over before she'd willingly choose to contact him.

Stephanie caught the quick gleam of amusement apparent, and deliberately arched an eyebrow in silent query, held it, then she accepted the card from his outstretched hand, careful to ensure their fingers didn't touch.

Was that an imperceptible quirk of mockery at the edge of his lips? She told herself she didn't give a damn.

Without a further word she turned and retraced her steps.

It was almost five, which allowed her one hour and ten minutes to collect Emma from the day care center, drive to Mermaid Beach, feed and bathe her daughter, then shower, dress, brief the baby-sitter and leave.

Do-able, provided there were no hiccups or delays.

An added bonus was that Sarah, her baby-sitter had offered to arrive early and take up any slack.

Something for which Stephanie was immensely grateful as she stepped into a slim-fitting black dress and slid the zip home. A few strokes of the brush to her strawberry-blond hair restored order to the stylish bob, and she examined her makeup, added a touch of blusher to her cheeks, spritzed her favorite Hermés perfume to several pulse points, then she slid her feet into stiletto-heeled black pumps, caught up a black shoulder bag and stepped quickly into the lounge.

'Bye, darling.' She leaned down and gave Emma a hug. 'Be a good girl for Sarah.' She turned toward the baby-sitter. 'Any problems, ring me on my cell phone. I won't be late. *Thanks,*' she added with heartfelt sincerity.

'Anytime. Enjoy yourself.'

That was debatable, Stephanie perceived as she crossed the path and slid in behind the wheel of her car.

Business, she reminded herself as she reversed out from the driveway, and eased the sedan down the quiet suburban street. Tonight is strictly business.

Why, then, did she have the feeling that she'd been very cleverly manipulated?

The distance between Mermaid Beach and the Sheraton Mirage hotel at Main Beach represented a fifteen-minute drive…slightly less, if she was fortunate enough to strike a green light at every traffic controlled intersection.

It was a beautiful summer evening, the sun reflected the day's heat, and Stephanie reached forward to adjust the air conditioning.

High-rise buildings stood like tall sentinels, vying with luxury hotels lining the long gently curved stretch of oceanfront.

The Gold Coast had been her home for almost four years. Years in which she'd mentally fought to put a broken relationship behind her and deal with the bitterness of knowing the man in her life had expected...no, begged, her to terminate an accidental pregnancy on the grounds a baby would represent too much responsibility and wreck his plans. With icy calm she'd handed back his engagement ring and walked out of his life.

It hadn't been easy. Yet Emma made it all worthwhile. She was a dear child, Stephanie's image with soft blond curls with the merest tinge of reddish gold.

A horn-blast shattered Stephanie's introspection, and a slight frown creased her forehead as the car developed a faint bump. Seconds later she didn't know whether to curse or cry as she pulled into the side of the road and brought the vehicle to a halt.

Just what she needed. A puncture, when she hadn't allowed herself a minute to spare. Dammit. She reached forward and popped the boot, then she slid out of her seat and prepared to change the tire. Left front, she determined as she removed the jack and set it in position.

Stiletto heels and a figure-hugging dress didn't make for ideal maneuvering. Nor did she relish wrestling with unfamiliar tools as she attempted to loosen stubborn wheel nuts.

This was one occasion when she was more than willing to put feminine self-sufficiency to one side and welcome male assistance.

Except no car stopped, and she battled with the task, completed the wheel change, replaced tools and then cleaned up as best she could with a packet of moist wipes and a box of tissues.

A quick glance at her watch confirmed she was already ten minutes late, and she reached for her cell phone, extracted Raoul Lanier's business card and keyed in the appropriate digits.

He answered on the second ring, and she identified herself, offered an explanation, an apology, and ended the call before he had the opportunity to say a further word.

Five minutes later Stephanie slid the car to a halt in the Sheraton Mirage hotel underground car park and took the lift to the main lobby.

She saw Raoul at once, his height and breadth of shoulder emphasized by superb tailoring, his dark hair well-groomed.

As she drew close he turned toward her, and he stood watching her approach with an unwavering scrutiny that made her want to check if there was a smudge on her nose or cheek, and wonder whether her hasty cleaning-up had removed every speck of grease and dust.

Stephanie mentally squared her shoulders as she summoned forth a warm smile. She was practiced in the social graces, and adept at handling any situation. It was very rare for her to allow anything or anyone to ruffle her composure.

All she had to do, she assured herself silently, was get through the next hour or two with her dignity intact.

'Sandrine. Michel,' she greeted with ease as she joined them. 'Raoul,' she acknowledged civilly. 'I'm sorry about the delay.'

Take control, a tiny voice prompted. 'Shall we go in?'

She didn't miss the faint narrowing of his dark eyes, nor did she mistake the deceptive indolence apparent, and she ignored the slight shiver that feathered its way down her spine.

Raoul Lanier was just a man whose wealth and power were enviable assets in the business arena. She had no interest in him on a personal level, she assured herself.

Why, then, did she feel on edge and about as confident as a seven-year-old child, instead of the twenty-seven-year-old woman she was?

CHAPTER TWO

THE maître 'd led them to a table with a splendid view out over the pool and ocean. He seated them with reserved politeness, then summoned the drinks waiter.

Stephanie perused the wine list with practiced ease. Her knowledge of Australian wines was comprehensive, and she conferred over a choice of red or white, sparkling or still.

'What would you suggest?' Raoul drawled, mildly amused by her determination to play hostess.

'The hotel carries a selection by a multigold medal vintner. I can recommend their Chardonnay or the Pinot Noir.'

Raoul ordered a bottle of each, and when the wine steward uncorked and presented the wine, Stephanie declined, opting for mineral water.

'The need for a clear head?'

'Of course,' she returned coolly. 'The evening's purpose is focused on discussions about marketing strategies for the movie.' She turned her attention to Michel. 'I trust you've had an opportunity to examine the paperwork?'

'Perhaps we could leave any business discussion until after we've ordered our starter and main?' Raoul suggested imperturbably.

Stephanie directed him a studied glance, and met his level gaze. 'If you'd prefer, Mr. Lanier.'

'Raoul,' he insisted silkily.

'Raoul,' she conceded, imitating his slightly accented intonation. If he wanted to play a game of verbal thrust and parry, she'd prove she could be his equal.

Her resolve deepened the color of her eyes and lent a slight tilt to her chin.

It amused and intrigued him. Most…no, *all,* he mentally amended, women of his acquaintance tended to assume a mantle of coquetry, some subtle, others distinctly blatant, in his presence. Cynicism acquired at a young age had taught him that wealth and social status provided the attraction. Experience hadn't changed his opinion.

A waiter approached their table, conferred over the choice of starters, and at a request from Michel, provided a knowledgeable dissertation regarding the merits of each main dish on the menu before taking their order.

Stephanie lifted her glass and sipped the contents. Despite the apparent social implications, this evening was *business,* and she intended to relay the pertinent aspects of marketing strategy, outline the precise course it would take for this particular film, then she would leave.

If Raoul, Michel and Sandrine chose to linger or move on to the bar, that was their choice.

She replaced her glass onto the table and directed her attention toward Michel. 'I've already outlined the major facets of film marketing strategy in an appendix among the paperwork handed to you this afternoon,' she began formally. She was aware of Raoul's studied gaze, and chose to ignore it.

'Briefly to recap, when the completed film is delivered to us from the studio, it receives a private viewing by several people, about thirty in all. Various meetings are held to discuss the target market, what age group the film will most appeal to, which segments should be selected for the trailer.' It was an involved process, and one in which she excelled. 'We need to determine which shots will appear in press releases to television and the media, overseas and locally.'

Raoul noted the way her skin took on a glow beneath the muted lighting, the small gestures she used to emphasis a point. The liking for her job seemed genuine, and her enthusiasm didn't appear to be contrived. Unless he was mistaken, this was no hard sell by a corporate executive intent on personal success at any price.

'In order to heighten public awareness of the film, we'll organize a fashion shoot with one or more of the prestige fashion magazines, and arrange coverage in at least two of the major national weekly magazines. As well as local and interstate newspapers.'

The waiter approached the table and set down their selected starters, and almost on cue the wine steward appeared to top up their drinks.

'It would be advantageous to utilize Sandrine's modeling connections to the fullest extent,'

Stephanie continued as she reached for her cutlery. 'We'll also arrange for you to be present at a few social events and organize media coverage. Press interviews will be set up with the main actors and a few of the cast, the release of which appear simultaneously to draw public attention to the film.'

'Impressive,' Michel drawled, incurring a sharp glance from his wife.

'Laudable,' Raoul inclined in agreement. 'Perhaps you'd care to elaborate—your degree of dedication to this particular project?'

'Total,' she responded, then qualified evenly, 'With one exception. In terms of personal family crisis, my daughter Emma takes precedence.'

'Not optimum,' Raoul discounted, employing an edge of ruthlessness.

A deliberate strategy to place her behind the eight ball? 'You have no obligations whatsoever, Mr. Lanier?' she posed smoothly. 'No wife or mistress who has license to your time?' Her gaze lanced his, level, unwavering, undeterred by the warning glint apparent. 'Or does *business* consume your life to the exclusion of all else?'

It was possible to hear a pin drop within the immediate vicinity of their table. No one, she imagined, had dared to confront Raoul Lanier in such a manner.

'A subtle query on your part?' Raoul posed with hateful amusement. 'As to whether I have a wife?'

'Your marital status is of no interest to me whatsoever,' she responded evenly. It was the truth. 'And you didn't answer the question.'

Would she be so brave if they were alone? Perhaps, he accorded silently, sufficiently intrigued to discover if the bravado was merely a facade.

'I allow myself leisure time.'

His drawled response set her teeth on edge, and she summoned a sweet smile. 'Sensible of you.'

She had no answer for the sensual tension electrifying the air between them. Or for the insane desire to challenge him to a verbal fencing match. It was almost as if some invisible imp was prompting her into battle, and putting words in her mouth she would normally never utter.

'I hope you weren't too inconvenienced in locating a baby-sitter at such short notice?' Sandrine queried in what Stephanie perceived as a skilled attempt to switch the subject of conversation.

'Fortunately not.'

Sandrine offered a wry smile. 'The Lanier brothers tend to snap their fingers and expect immediate action.'

'So I gather,' Stephanie responded dryly.

'Can I persuade you to try some wine, Stephanie?' Michel intervened smoothly. 'Half a glass won't affect your ability to drive.'

'Thank you, no.'

The waiter unobtrusively removed their plates, inquired if the starter was to their satisfaction, then retreated.

Raoul leaned back in his chair and subjected Stephanie to an analytical appraisal. The subdued lighting emphasized delicate bone structure, lent a soft glow to her skin and accentuated the blue depth of her eyes.

She possessed a lush mouth, full and softly curved, and he watched it draw in slightly, caught the faint tightening of muscles at the edge of her jaw as she became aware of his deliberate assessment.

For one infinitesimal second her eyes blazed fire, and he noted the imperceptible movement as she attempted to minimize a convulsive swallow.

Not so controlled, he decided with satisfaction, aware that it would provide an interesting challenge to explore the exigent chemistry between them.

How would that mouth feel beneath the pressure of his own? There was a part of him that wanted to ruffle her composure, test the level of her restraint, and handle the aftermath.

Stephanie barely restrained the impulse to *hit* him. He was deliberately needling her, like a supine panther who'd sighted a prey within reach and was toying with the decision to pounce, or play. Either way, the result would be the same.

Raoul Lanier was in for a surprise if he thought he could try those tactics with her, she decided in silent anger.

She held his gaze deliberately, and saw one eyebrow lift in a slow arch, almost as if he had read her mind. Mental telepathy? Somehow she doubted he possessed that ability. More likely it stemmed from an innate and accurate knowledge of women.

The appearance of the waiter with their main course temporarily diverted her attention. She looked at the plate placed before her, and felt her appetite diminish to zero.

'The meal isn't to your liking?'

Stephanie heard Raoul's deep drawl, sensed the double entendre, and for a brief moment she entertained tossing the contents of her glass in his face.

Smile, a tiny voice urged. This isn't the first occasion you've had to deal with male arrogance, and it sure won't be the last. Business was the purpose for this meeting, albeit that it was being conducted in luxurious surroundings with the accompaniment of fine food and wine.

'Do you have any queries?' she asked of Michel, and incurred his thoughtful gaze.

'You appear to have covered everything for the moment.'

'Perhaps Stephanie would care to give us her personal opinion on this film,' Raoul drawled as he toyed with his wineglass.

'My expertise is with marketing strategy, Mr. Lanier,' she said with grave politeness, whereas underneath that superficial veneer she was seething.

His gaze seemed to lance through every protective barrier she erected, and she hated him for it.

'Surely you have an opinion?' he queried mildly.

'Nothing is a guaranteed success,' she voiced steadily. 'And there are varied degrees of success. I understand both director and producer have a certain reputation in their field, the cast comprises relatively high profile actors, the theme will attract public interest.' Her gaze was unwavering as she held his. 'I can only assure you marketing will do a commendable job with promotion.'

She glimpsed his cynical smile, saw the hardness in those powerful features and refused to allow either to unsettle her equilibrium.

'A standard response,' Raoul acknowledged silkily. 'That conveys precisely nothing.'

She'd had enough. 'You're talking to the wrong person, Mr. Lanier. But then, you know that, don't you? This so-called business dinner is merely a social occasion initiated by you for your own amusement.' She removed her napkin and placed it beside her plate, then she stood to her feet and collected her evening purse. Ignoring Raoul, she focused her attention on Michel. 'Enjoy your meal.'

Without a further word she turned from the table and made her way to the main desk. Requesting the bill, she produced her corporate card, instructed the maximum estimated amount for the total be written in, then she signed the credit slip and pocketed her copy.

Stephanie moved into the foyer and crossed to the lift, jabbing the Call button with more force than necessary.

Damn Raoul Lanier. He'd succeeded in getting beneath her skin, and she hated him for it. Hated herself for allowing him to affect her in a way that tore at the foundations of unbiased *professional* good manners.

For heaven's sake, where was the lift? Another five seconds, and she'd take the stairs. Almost on

command, the doors slid open, four people emerged
and Stephanie stepped into the cubicle, then turned
toward the control panel.

Only to freeze at the sight of Raoul Lanier on the
verge of entering the lift.

'What do you think you're doing?' she managed
to ask in a furious undertone.

'Accompanying you down to your car.' He
reached forward and depressed the button designat-
ing the car park.

An action which galvanized Stephanie into jabbing
the button that held the doors open. 'Something
that's totally unnecessary. Get out.'

He didn't answer. Instead he leaned forward, captured both her hands and held them firmly while he
depressed the appropriate button.

Stephanie wrenched against his grasp in an attempt
to get free, without success, and she watched with
mounting anger as the doors slid closed and the lift
began to descend.

'Let go of me.' Her voice was as cool as an arctic
floe.

'When the lift reaches the car park,' Raoul
drawled imperturbably.

'You are the most arrogant, insolent, insufferable
man I've ever had the misfortune to meet.'

'Really? I'm flattered. I expected at least ten
damning descriptions.'

'Give me a few seconds,' she threatened darkly.

She was supremely conscious of him, his physical
height and breadth, the aura of power he exuded, and

this close his choice of cologne teased her senses, notwithstanding the essence of the man and the electric tension evident between them.

The heightened sensuality was almost a tangible entity, powerful, primeval, riveting. It made her afraid. Not only of him, but herself and the long dormant emotions she'd deliberately tamped down for four years.

The lift came to a smooth halt, and she wrenched her hands free, then exited the cubicle the instant the doors slid open.

'Where is your car?'

She began walking toward the glass doors that led to the car park. 'There's no need to play the gentleman. The area is well-lit.'

She may as well have not spoken, and she drew in a deep breath, releasing it slowly as she deliberately ignored him and increased her pace.

It took only minutes to reach her car, and she extracted her keys, unlocked the door, then stilled as a hand prevented her from sliding in behind the wheel.

'Whatever you're thinking of doing,' she said tightly, searing him with a look that would have felled a lesser man. 'Don't.'

'I was going to offer an apology.'

'For initiating an unnecessary social occasion in the guise of *business,* then conducting a deliberate game of cat and mouse with me?' Her tone was deceptively soft, but her eyes resembled crystalline sapphire. 'An apology is merely words, Mr. Lanier, and I find your manner unacceptable.' She looked pointedly at his hand. 'You have three seconds to walk away. Otherwise I'll alert security.'

'And request you rejoin me at dinner,' he continued as if she hadn't spoken.

'I'm no longer hungry, I don't like you, and—' she paused fractionally, and aimed for the kill '—the last thing I want to do is spend another minute in your company. Is that clear?'

Raoul inclined his head in mocking acceptance. 'Perfectly.' He attended to the clasp and held open the door. *'Au revoir.'*

Stephanie slid in behind the wheel, inserted the key into the ignition and fired the engine. 'Goodbye.'

The instant he closed the door she reversed out of the parking bay, then without sparing him a glance she drove toward the exit.

Minutes later she joined the flow of traffic traveling toward the center of town, and it wasn't until she'd cleared the three major intersections that she allowed herself to reflect on the scene in the hotel car park.

She'd managed to have the last word, but somehow she had the feeling Raoul Lanier had deliberately contrived his apparent defeat. And that annoyed the heck out of her!

'You're home early,' Sarah said with surprise when Stephanie entered the house just before nine.

'Everything all right?' Stephanie asked as she placed her bag down onto the table, and began removing her earrings.

'Fine. Emma is never any trouble. She had a glass

of milk at seven-thirty, and went to bed without a murmur.'

She looked at the textbooks laid out on the table, the empty coffee mug. 'Another coffee? I'm making myself some.'

Sarah stood, closed and stacked her books, then slid them into a soft briefcase. 'Thanks, but I'll take a rain check.'

'I appreciate your coming over at such short notice.'

'It's a pleasure,' the baby-sitter declared warmly. 'You have a lovely quiet house, perfect study conditions.' She grinned, then rolled her eyes expressively. 'Two teenage brothers tend to make a lot of noise.'

Stephanie extracted some bills from her purse and pressed them into the girl's hand. 'Thanks, Sarah. Good luck with the exams.'

She saw her out the door, then she locked up and went to check on Emma.

The child was sleeping, her expression peaceful as she clutched a favorite rag doll to her chest. Stephanie leaned down and adjusted the covers, then lightly pushed back a stray lock of hair that had fallen forward onto one soft cheek.

The tug of unconditional love consumed her. Nothing, *nothing* was as wonderful as the gift of a child. Emma's happiness and well-being was worth any sacrifice. A stressful job, the need to present cutting-edge marketing strategy, estimating consumer appeal and ensuring each project was a winner.

The necessity, she added wryly, to occasionally entertain outside conventional business hours. She was familiar with an entire range of personality traits. In her line of business, she came into contact with them all.

Yet no man had managed to get beneath her skin the way Raoul Lanier did. She dealt with men who'd made flirting an art form. Men who imagined wealth condoned dubious behavior and an appalling lack of manners. Then there were those who had so many tickets on themselves they no longer knew who they were.

She'd handled each and every one of them with tact and diplomacy. Even charm. None of which qualities were evident in the presence of a certain Frenchman.

He unsettled her. Far too much for her own liking. She didn't want to *feel* insecure and vulnerable. She'd tread that path once before. She had no intention of retracing her steps.

Stephanie entered the main bedroom, carefully removed her dress and slipped off her shoes, then she cleansed her face free of makeup, stripped off her underwear and donned a long cotton T-shirt before returning to collect her mug of coffee and sink into a deep-cushioned chair in front of the television.

At ten she turned out the lights and went to bed, only to lay awake staring into the darkness as she fought to dismiss Raoul Lanier's disturbing image.

*   *   *

The in-house phone buzzed, and Stephanie automatically reached for it, depressed the button and endeavored to tame the frustrated edge to her voice. 'Yes. What is it, Isabel?'

It wasn't shaping up to be a good day. That little Irish gremlin, Murphy, had danced a jig on her turf from the moment she woke. Water from the shower ran cold from the hot tap, necessitating a call to a plumber. Emma wanted porridge instead of cereal, then requested egg with toast cut into soldiers, only to take two mouthfuls and refuse to eat anymore. Depositing her daughter at day care resulted in an unprecedented tantrum, and she tore a nail wrestling the punctured tire from her boot at the tire mart en route to work.

'I have a delivery for you out front.'

'Whatever it is, take care of it.'

'Flowers with a card addressed to you?'

Flowers? No one sent her flowers, except on special occasions. And today wasn't one of them. 'Okay, I'm on my way to reception.'

Roses. Tight buds in cream, peach and pale apricot. Two, no three dozen. Long-stemmed, encased in cellophane, with a subtle delicate perfume.

'Stephanie Sommers? Please sign the delivery slip for this envelope.'

Who would send her such an expensive gift? Even as the query formed in her mind, her mouth tightened at the possible answer.

He wouldn't...would he?

'They're beautiful,' Isabel breathed with envy as

Stephanie detached an accompanying envelope and plucked out the card.

"A small token to atone for last night. R."

Each word seemed to leap out in stark reminder, and she wanted to shove Raoul Lanier's *token* into the nearest wastepaper bin. *Atone? Twenty* dozen roses wouldn't atone for the studied arrogance of the man.

'Shall I fetch a vase?'

Stephanie drew a shallow breath, then released it. 'Yes.' She handed the large cellophane sheaf to her secretary. 'Place these on the front desk.'

'You don't want them in your office?'

'They'll make me sneeze.' A slight fabrication, but she didn't want to be constantly reminded of the man who'd gifted them. 'Take messages on any of my calls for the rest of the afternoon, unless they're urgent, or from Emma's day care center.'

She stepped back into her office, closed the door, then crossed to her desk, picked up the letter opener and slit the envelope.

Quite what she expected to find, she wasn't sure. Certainly it had to be relatively important to warrant special delivery.

Stephanie extracted the slim piece of paper, saw that it was a check, made out to her and signed by Raoul Lanier for an amount that covered the cost of dinner the previous evening. To endorse it, just in case she might be in doubt, there was a hotel business card attached with his name written on the reverse side.

How dare he? The dinner was a legitimate business expense. Raoul Lanier had chosen to make it personal.

Well, she knew just what to do with his check. Her fingers moved automatically, and seconds later the torn pieces fluttered into the wastepaper bin.

Stephanie sank into her chair and turned on the screen on her computer. *Work.* She had plenty of it. All she had to do was immerse herself in the electronic checking of pertinent details to dispense the omnipotent Frenchman from her mind.

Except it didn't quite work out that way. His image intruded, disrupting her focus, minimizing her concentration.

It was something of an endurance feat that she completed the day's schedule without mishap, and she closed down the computer as Isabel entered with a sheaf of messages. Three of which she returned, two were put to one side for the morning, and one she discarded.

Raoul Lanier could whistle *Dixie,* she decided vengefully as she slid papers into her briefcase and caught up her bag.

Her gaze skimmed the office in a cursory check before leaving for the evening. She caught sight of the special delivery envelope that had contained Raoul Lanier's check, and she reached for it, flipped it idly between her fingers, then on impulse she bent down and caught up the torn check she'd consigned to the wastepaper bin.

Stephanie took an envelope from her stationery

drawer, placed the torn check into it, dampened the seal, then wrote Raoul Lanier in bold black ink, followed by the name of his hotel.

The Sheraton wasn't that far out of her way, and a wry smile teased her lips as she anticipated his expression when he opened the envelope.

Tit for tat wasn't an enviable modus operandi, but she was darned if she'd allow him to have the upper hand.

It was a simple matter to drive up to the main hotel entrance and hand the addressed envelope to the concierge. Difficult to hide a vaguely exultant smile as she eased the car onto the main road.

Traffic was heavy, consequently it took at least three light changes to pass through each main intersection as she headed for the day care center.

Emma looked slightly flushed, and her eyes held a brightness that foreshadowed an increased temperature. 'I'll see how she fares through the night,' Stephanie declared quietly to the attendant nursing sister. 'I may keep her home tomorrow.'

'Give me a call in the morning.'

An hour later she'd bathed and changed Emma, encouraged her to eat a little dinner, only to have her throw up soon after. Something that occurred with regularity throughout the night.

By morning they were both tired and wan, and at eight Stephanie made a series of calls that gained a doctor's appointment, the office to relay she'd be working from home and to divert any phone calls to her message bank and finally, the day care center.

'Sick,' Emma said in a forlorn voice, and Stephanie leaned down to brush her lips across her daughter's forehead.

'I know, sweetheart. We'll go see the doctor soon, and get some medicine to make you better.'

Washing. Loads of it. She took the second completed load out and pushed it into the drier, then systematically filled the washing machine and set it going again.

A gastro virus, the doctor pronounced, and prescribed treatment and care. Stephanie called into the pharmacy, collected a few essentials from the nearby supermarket, then she drove home and settled Emma comfortably on the sofa with one of her favorite videos slotted into the VCR.

A sophisticated laptop linked her to the office, and she noted the calls logged in on her message bank, then settled down to work.

Emma slept for an hour, had some chicken broth, a dry piece of toast, then snuggled down in the makeshift bed Stephanie set up on the couch.

By evening Emma was much improved, and she slept through the night without mishap. Even so, Stephanie decided to keep her home another day as a precaution.

Work was a little more difficult with a reasonably energetic child underfoot, and when she'd settled Emma into bed for her afternoon nap she crossed to the phone and made a series of necessary calls.

One revealed the information she sought, in that Michel Lanier was investing personal, not Lanier corporate funds. Therefore it was solely Michel to whom she owed professional allegiance.

Stephanie opened her laptop, and began sourcing the necessary data she needed to complete a report. Although film was her area of expertise, she worked on other marketing projects and liaised with several of her associates.

It was almost three when the doorbell rang, and she quickly crossed to open the door before whoever was on the other side could ring the bell again.

Security was an important feature for a single woman living alone with a young child, and aluminum grills covered every window and both doors.

Possibly it was a neighbor, or a hawker canvassing door-to-door.

Stephanie unlocked the paneled wooden door and was temporarily unable to contain her surprise at the sight of Raoul Lanier's tall frame beyond the aperture.

He looked vital, dynamic, his broad-boned features portraying a handsome ruggedness that was primitive, compelling. Almost barbaric.

Words formed to demand how he'd discovered where she lived. Then they died before they found voice. All Raoul Lanier had to do was lift the telephone and make a few inquiries to elicit the pertinent information.

CHAPTER THREE

'WHAT are you doing here?'

Raoul arched an eyebrow. 'Do you usually greet everyone this way?'

'No,' she managed to say coolly.

'And keep them standing on the doorstep?'

He bothered her more than she was prepared to admit. On a professional level, she had no recourse but to suffer his presence. However, this was *her* time, her *home*, which made it very personal.

She was safe. The outer wrought-iron security door was locked. He couldn't enter unless she chose to release the catch.

'I conduct business in my office, Mr. Lanier. I suggest you contact my secretary and make an appointment.'

'In case it slipped your mind, you refused to take my call.'

'I had to do some urgent work on the computer,' she explained, determined not to sound defensive. 'My secretary took messages.'

'I gave her one. You didn't return it.'

She regarded him carefully. 'There was no need, given Michel is investing personal, not Lanier company funds, into the film.'

'As a matter of interest, did the roses make it into your office?'

Stephanie's eyes flared, then assumed cool control. 'I had Isabel put them in reception.'

'And tore up my check.'

'It was a business dinner,' she reminded firmly.

'Business was on the agenda,' Raoul granted in measured tones.

'It was the sole reason I accepted your invitation.'

There was cynical amusement lurking in the depths of his eyes. 'You have since made that remarkably clear.'

'I'm not into playing word-games, nor do I indulge in male ego-stroking.'

He laughed. A deep throaty sound that held a degree of spontaneous humor, and something else she didn't care to define.

'Invite me in, Stephanie.'

'No. Emma is due to wake from her nap anytime soon.'

'Have dinner with me tonight.'

'I don't date, Mr. Lanier,' she added icily.

'Raoul,' he insisted evenly. 'The sharing of a meal doesn't necessarily constitute a date.'

He really was too much! 'What part of *no* don't you understand?' she demanded, and saw his eyes narrow slightly.

'Are you so afraid of me?'

Fear had many aspects, and while her personal safety wasn't in question, her emotional sanity was something else entirely. She'd turned the lock on her emotional heart and thrown away the key. This man saw too much, sensed too much, and was therefore dangerous.

'You're wasting your time,' she said quietly.

One eyebrow arched. 'You think so?'

'We have nothing to discuss.'

'Yes,' Raoul argued silkily. 'We do.'

His gaze seemed to sear right through to her soul, and it took enormous willpower to keep her eyes level, *emotionless.*

'In your dreams,' Stephanie reiterated with pseudo sweetness.

His expression didn't change, although his voice was a soft drawl that conveyed innate knowledge. *'Oui.'*

She drew a deep breath, and released it slowly. 'If you don't leave immediately, I'll make a call and have you charged with harassment.'

Stephanie closed the door, and leaned against it for several long minutes, then she drew in a deep breath and moved toward the kitchen. Crossing to the refrigerator she took a can of cola, popped the tab, then she extracted a glass and filled it with the sparkling dark liquid.

Her skin felt heated, and her pulse beat fast at the edge of her throat. Damn him. Who did he think he was?

A hollow laugh escaped into the silence of the room. Raoul Lanier knew exactly who he was. What's more, she had the instinctive feeling he would stop at nothing to get what he wanted.

The question was, *what* did Raoul Lanier want with her?

Sex. Why else did men pursue women, if not to indulge in intimacy?

Hadn't she discovered that to her cost? Ben had said the sweet words and pushed all the right buttons. Until she fell pregnant. Then he became someone she didn't know at all, and she'd walked away, vowing never to trust a man again, ever.

There were men she dealt with in the course of her business life, and despite numerous invitations she'd held steadfast to her rule not to date.

However none had affected her as Raoul Lanier did. Instant awareness. Sexual chemistry at its zenith, she added with silent cynicism.

Electric, primeval, *shocking,* she acknowledged, remembering vividly the moment their gazes met when he'd walked into her office.

Within seconds, it had seemed as if her life came to a standstill and there was only *him.* Invading her senses, warming her blood, staking a claim. As if he possessed a blueprint to her future. It had unnerved her then. It disturbed and unnerved her now.

Her fingers clenched until the knuckles shone white, and she crossed to the sink and discarded the glass.

Do something. Anything. The ironing, she decided. Heaven knew she had enough of it. By then Emma would be awake, and she'd entertain her until it was time to cook dinner.

Two hours later Stephanie settled Emma in front

of the television and slid an educational video into the VCR.

'I'll start dinner, sweetheart.' The house favored open-plan living, and the lounge adjoined the dining room, both of which were visible from the kitchen.

There was chicken and vegetable broth left from yesterday, and she peeled potatoes, carrots and added broccoli to go with the steamed chicken. Better to stick to something fairly bland for the next day or two.

She had just added water to the saucepan when she heard the singsong peal of the doorbell. She reached for the kitchen towel, dried her hands and crossed into the lounge.

'Doorbell,' Emma announced solemnly as Stephanie moved into the hallway.

The only person who popped in without forewarning was her neighbor, and she opened the door with a ready smile, only to have it fade as she recognized the man on the landing.

'What are you doing here?'

'I believe we've already done that,' Raoul said with musing mockery. He held out two brown paper sacks. 'I brought dinner.'

'Why?' she demanded baldly.

'Why not?' he posed lightly.

'Mommy?'

Stephanie closed her eyes, then opened them again, spearing him with a look that spoke volumes before turning toward her daughter. 'It's okay, darling,' she said gently. 'Go back into the lounge. I'll be there in a minute.'

'Hello, Emma.'

His voice was calm, soothing…friendly, *warm*, damn him!

'Hello.' Emma was openly curious, and not at all intimidated. 'Who are you?'

Raoul sank down onto his haunches in one fluid movement. 'A friend of your mother's.'

'What's your name?'

'Raoul.'

'Are you having dinner with us?' the little girl queried solemnly.

'Would you like me to?'

Oh my, he was good! Stephanie shot him a glance that would have felled a lesser man.

'Yes.'

Unfair, she wanted to scream.

'Mommy?'

'I'm sure Raoul—' she hesitated fractionally over his name '—has plans for the evening.'

'Do you?' Emma asked, her eyes wide with curiosity.

'No plans,' Raoul assured.

Dammit, he was enjoying this!

'You can watch my video,' Emma invited, offering a generous smile.

'I'd like that.'

Stephanie met his eyes, glimpsed the silent query lurking there and wanted nothing more than to close the door in his face. 'I don't think it would be a good idea.'

'I promise to be on my best behavior,' Raoul declared solemnly.

Don't you get it? she wanted to demand in anger. You're *not* welcome. And never will be, a silent voice echoed.

He inclined his head, aware that she was teetering on the edge, and anything he said at this point could work to his disadvantage.

'Please, Mommy.'

Blind trust. To a child, everything was simple. If only it was as simple for an adult!

Stephanie inserted the key and unlocked the security door. 'Come in.' Her voice was polite, but lacked any pretense of enthusiasm or graciousness.

'You're big,' Emma declared as he entered the lobby, and he smiled.

'Maybe it's because you're small.'

'I'm three,' the little girl pronounced proudly.

Raoul indicated the paper sacks. 'If you lead the way, I'll deposit these in the kitchen.'

It was a comfortable one-level house, relatively modern with average-size rooms. Raoul's presence seemed to diminish them, and she was supremely conscious of him as he followed her down the hallway.

It was almost as if all her fine body hairs stood on end in involuntary protection. Which was crazy, she silently chastised. Already she was fast becoming a mass of nerves, and he hadn't even touched her.

What would you do if he did? Don't think about it. It's not going to happen.

She crossed around behind the kitchen counter in an unconscious attempt to put some space between them.

There was already two saucepans simmering on the stove, and she indicated them as he placed the sacks down. 'I usually feed Emma about this time.'

'Then perhaps we can eat together.'

Stephanie opened one sack, and removed plastic containers that revealed tandoori chicken, steamed rice and a selection of vegetables. The second sack contained a crusty baguette, a selection of cheeses and a bottle of wine.

It offered a tasty feast, and surpassed the broth, boiled chicken and plain vegetables she'd intended to share with Emma.

'I'll fetch an extra plate and cutlery.'

'Tell me where they are, and I'll attend to it while you set out the food.'

'You can sit next to me,' Emma said in a bright voice.

Oh Emma, *don't.* This is a one-off, not the beginning of a friendship.

'It will be a pleasure.'

'I'm a big girl now. I can eat all by myself.'

It was meaningless chatter, and Stephanie didn't know whether to smile or sigh as her daughter regaled their reluctantly invited guest with the names of her friends at the day care center, her swimming lessons, a recent birthday party, videos she liked to watch and the much anticipated event…a trip to the theme park Movieworld on Saturday.

'Mommy's got tickets,' Emma assured as she finished the last of her vegetables. 'You can come, too.'

Oh, no, he can't. 'Mr. Lanier is a very busy man, darling. Besides, you may not be well enough to go,' Stephanie qualified quickly. 'We'll have to wait and see.'

She didn't want to spend time with him, even in the company of her daughter. And he knew. She could sense the faint amusement evident as she stood to her feet and began collecting plates and cutlery together.

'You can watch my video with me while Mommy does the dishes.' Emma began to hop down from the chair, then she paused. 'Please leave the table, Mommy?'

Stephanie felt her heart tug at Emma's earnest attempt to remember her manners. 'Yes,' she said gently, watching as her daughter unhesitatingly accepted Raoul Lanier's hand.

How could Emma be so friendly with someone she'd only just met? A man, when Emma came into contact with so few men. *Especially a man of Raoul Lanier's caliber.* Someone Stephanie had disliked on sight.

Dislike wasn't an adequate description, she decided cynically as she crossed to the sink and began rinsing plates.

His mere presence attacked the protective wall she'd built around herself. She liked to think she had total control, and responsibility for her life and everything in it rested solely with *her*. She didn't need a man invading her space, her time, her emotions.

Unless, of course, a woman was sufficiently fortunate to find the right man. Someone who would recognize and respect a woman's needs, who would give as well as take.

Get a grip, a skeptical voice derided silently. You're content with the status quo, remember? You have a home, a good job and a child who is the light of your life. What more do you want?

Nothing, she assured herself, and knew she lied.

The rinsed plates and cutlery were consigned to the dishwasher, and she dealt with the saucepans with more diligence than was necessary.

Stephanie reentered the lounge and almost halted midstep at the sight of Emma seated beside the man she wished was anywhere else but *here*.

They looked *comfortable* with each other, and she wasn't sure she liked it. Be honest, and admit you hate it, an inner voice taunted.

What's more, Emma was giving Raoul a running commentary on the video as it played, drawing his attention to the various figures in and out of costume.

A glance at the screen was sufficient for Stephanie to determine the video had only a few minutes left to run, and as the credits rolled Stephanie reached for her daughter's hand as she deactivated the VCR. 'Time for your bath, sweetheart.'

For a moment it seemed Emma might object, then she slid off the cushioned seat and stood.

'I'll come back and say good-night,' she assured Raoul with childish earnestness as he unwound his length in one fluid movement.

'Mr. Lanier has to leave,' Stephanie said firmly, willing him to do just that. Her voice gentled, 'You'd better say good-night now.'

Emma looked at him with unblinking solemnity for all of twenty seconds. 'Good night.'

Stephanie began to lead her daughter from the room, only to have Emma pause and ask wistfully,

'Will you come and see us again?'

Raoul looked from the child to the mother, and back again. His smile was gentle. 'I'd like that.'

Emma grinned unabashedly, and broke into a skipping gait as she followed Stephanie from the room.

Oh hell, Stephanie cursed silently as she ran water into the bath and began undressing her daughter. How did you tell a three-year-old not to like someone? Explain that adult judgment was based on more than superficial appearance? And the reason for her mother's dislike was seeded in distrust and fear?

It was far beyond the comprehension of a child, and because of that it would be unfair to issue a reprimand.

Raoul focused his attention on the number of picture frames lining a mahogany dropped table, and moved close to examine them.

Emma as a baby; sitting clutching a teddy bear that was almost of a similar size to the child; standing; perched on Santa Claus's knee in a store studio shot; seated on a tricycle.

There was a photo of an older couple whom he deduced were Stephanie's parents, but nothing of the man who was Emma's father.

He lifted a hand and threaded fingers through his hair. If he had any sense he'd let himself out of the house and drive back to his hotel where at least three hours' work awaited him on the laptop. He had international telephone calls to make, data to check. He'd be lucky if he got to bed before midnight.

Not that it mattered much, he reflected wryly. The past few nights hadn't been given to peaceful sleep. His mind had centered too often on a strawberry-blond blue-eyed young marketing executive who held no qualms in challenging him to a verbal sparring match at the slightest provocation.

His gaze strayed to the television, caught the moving images in color and endeavored to focus his attention on a geographical program featuring a safari park in Africa.

The sound of a childish voice had him turning toward the door, and seconds later Emma skipped into the room ahead of Stephanie.

'I'm going to bed now.'

She was her mother in miniature. The hair was a few shades lighter, but the eyes were bright blue, and the features held the promise of fine bone structure.

'Good night, Emma.'

'I'll see you out before I put Emma down,' Stephanie ventured coolly.

'If you trust me in your kitchen, I'll make coffee

while you put Emma to bed. There's something I want to discuss with you.'

She didn't believe him. He could see the faint wariness, the doubt. And the need not to make an undue fuss in front of her daughter.

'I'll be back in ten minutes,' she accorded with resignation. 'Coffee and sugar are in the pantry. Milk in the refrigerator. I take mine white with one sugar.'

She reentered the lounge to find two cups filled with steaming coffee set on the occasional table, and the aroma of freshly ground coffee beans teased her nostrils.

'You've made a conquest,' Stephanie indicated as she picked up a cup.

Raoul inclined his head. 'With Emma,' he acknowledged in an accented drawl. 'But not her mother.'

'Nor are you likely to,' she assured coolly. There was a part of her that silently screamed for him to leave, *now*. She didn't want him in her house, her lounge, and she especially didn't want him creating havoc with her emotional sanity.

He didn't shift position, yet there was a stillness evident in his stance, an intense watchful quality that sent prickles of alarm scudding down the length of her spine. 'No?'

One single word that held a wealth of meaning she didn't want to explore. 'Why don't you cut to the chase?' A bald suggestion that evoked a cynical smile.

'Your unbiased opinion on the projected success of the movie Michel is investing in.'

'I wouldn't hazard a guess,' Stephanie offered evenly. 'There are too many dependent factors.' Her gaze speared his. 'Now, if you don't mind, I must ask you to leave. I have a report I need to work on.'

A lazy smile curved his mouth. 'A businesslike indication the evening is at an end?'

'Yes.' She wrestled with her conscience, and added, 'It was thoughtful of you to bring dinner. Thank you.'

'How polite.'

She detected mockery in his tone, and ignored it as she led the way toward the front door. There was a heightened awareness that played havoc with her nerve endings. Dammit, she could almost *feel* his presence as he walked in her wake, and she hated her reaction as much as she hated *him*.

Stephanie slipped the latch, opened the door and stood to one side to allow him clear passage. 'Good night, Mr. Lanier.'

'Raoul,' he insisted quietly. 'There is just one more thing.'

'What?' she managed to ask with remarkable steadiness.

'This.'

His hands captured her face and his head lowered down to hers before she could utter any protest, and then it was too late, for his mouth had taken possession of her own in a kiss that was so incredibly evocative it stirred her emotions and sent them rocketing out of control.

Dear heaven. It was all she could do not to lean in against him as he deepened the kiss to something so intensely sensual her whole body quivered in reaction.

This is *insane,* a tiny voice cautioned. What in hell are you *doing?*

With determined resolve she reached up and wrenched free of his hands, his tantalizing mouth, at the same time taking an unsteady step backward in an attempt to put some space between them.

Her breathing came in ragged gasps, and she could only stand looking at him with a combination of dismay and shock.

She wanted to scream *how dare you?* Twin flags of color tinged her cheeks, and her eyes darkened to the deepest sapphire. 'Get out.'

The words emerged in a damning whisper, and he pressed a finger to her mouth, tracing its slightly swollen curves with a gentleness that almost undid her.

'Au revoir, cherie.'

He stepped past her, and she closed the door, attached the safety chain, then she turned and leaned her back against the solid wood.

She closed her eyes against his image, then opened them again. As much as she blamed *him,* she also apportioned herself some of the blame. For not only responding, but *enjoying* the feel of that skillful mouth as it possessed her own.

Stephanie pushed herself away from the door and collected the empty coffee cups from the lounge and carried them into the kitchen.

Menial chores completed, she entered the small room she'd set up as a home office, activated her laptop and spent three hours on the report.

It was late when she went to bed, and after two hours spent tossing and turning, she switched on the bed lamp and read for an hour before falling into a deep sleep filled with a vivid dream about a night-marish character who bore a striking resemblance to Raoul Lanier.

CHAPTER FOUR

THE weekends were strictly devoted to mother-and-daughter time. Saturday morning Stephanie put Emma in the car and drove to a park with a play area, grassy banks bordering a meandering ornamental lake where children could feed the ducks.

For more than an hour Emma ran and played with some of the other children, scrambled over the jungle gym and had several turns on the swing.

Then it was time to drive to the local shopping center, collect the week's groceries before returning home for lunch. While Emma had her afternoon nap, Stephanie caught up with the housework, after which Emma engaged in swimming lessons held at the local pool.

Stephanie inevitably planned something special for dinner, and when the dishes had been cleared away and Emma was bathed and in bed, she'd curl up in a chair and slot a rented video into the VCR.

The pattern rarely changed, and she told herself she was content. Or she had been, until five days ago when a tall ruggedly attractive man with a fascinating French accent invaded her life.

Last night his touch had awakened feelings and emotions she didn't want to think about. Yet conversely, they infiltrated her mind and upset her equilibrium.

Stephanie let her thoughts wander from the actors on screen depicting unrequited love between two people from opposite ends of the social structure.

Another week, she determined, then the film would wrap. That was when her job would step into a higher gear as she organized television interviews, photo and fashion shoots, and the pièce de résistance, the gala dinner and dance.

Her involvement with Michel and Sandrine would be at a premium. Her contact with Raoul would hopefully be minimal.

Then Michel, Sandrine and Raoul would fly out from the Gold Coast to New York, Paris…and her life would revert to normal.

Sunday brought the coveted visit to Movieworld, and Stephanie took pleasure in seeing all the sights, experiencing the acted thrills and spills through the eyes of her daughter. Emma could barely keep awake toward the end, and after such an exciting day she willingly had her bath, ate an early dinner, then climbed into bed.

Monday brought a return to their weekday routine, and Stephanie focused on her schedule as she checked and wrote up her diary.

A cocktail party on Tuesday evening, followed by the gala dinner Saturday night meant she needed to enlist Sarah's baby-sitting services, and she made the call.

The day fled swiftly, the afternoon proving fraught

as last-minute checks revealed a few glitches she needed to chase up and eliminate. Her car, which she'd dropped in for its customary service, needed a replacement part that hadn't arrived by courier in time for the mechanic to finish the job. A temporary loaned vehicle sufficed, and when she arrived home it was to discover a stray dog...a very large dog, she surmised, had somehow gained entrance through the day and had dug up nearly all of her garden plants. He'd also scared their cat half to death judging by his perch high up a tree.

Adding insult to injury, the dog had had a ball trying to drag washing from the clothesline.

It should have been Friday the thirteenth, Stephanie muttered beneath her breath as she set about rescuing the cat, gathering up broken plants, then she retrieved the washing and sorted clothes into Mend, Discard, Wash.

Surprisingly she slept well and woke to a beautifully sunny day with the promise of soaring temperatures and high humidity.

Stephanie favored slim-fitting stylish business suits for office wear, and she owned several that she mixed and matched with a variety of silk blouses. She coveted a sophisticated look, actively promoting an image of skilled efficiency, knowledge, nous.

This morning she selected a tailored skirt and jacket in deep sapphire blue. No blouse, black stiletto heels, her only jewelry a watch and slender neck chain.

The day progressed without a hitch, and she arrived home with forty minutes in which to bathe and feed Emma, shower, dress, then leave at six to attend an invitation-only cocktail party held in a very prestigious penthouse apartment at Main Beach.

Speed and organization were of the essence, and not for the first time she wished she had an eight-hour-a-day job that began when she walked through the office door in the morning and ended when she left late afternoon. And after-hours social obligations didn't form part of her salary package.

If that were the case, she wouldn't be able to afford this pleasantly furnished brick and tile house with its swimming pool, situated a short walk from the beach and a major shopping center. Nor would she own a relatively late-model car, or possess such a fashionable wardrobe of clothes.

For some reason she viewed the evening's cocktail party with unaccustomed reluctance. She need only stay a short while, she reminded herself as she put the finishing touches to her makeup, then she added earrings, a matching pendant, and slipped her feet into black stiletto-heeled pumps.

Basic black in a classic design, Stephanie accorded as she checked her appearance in the long cheval mirror. Short sleeves, scooped neckline, smooth-fitting, with black lace overlaying the skirt and finishing in a scalloped hemline a modest few inches above the knee.

She flicked a glance at her wristwatch, caught up her evening purse and walked out into the lounge where Sarah was entertaining Emma with a new picture storybook.

The little girl had already been bathed and fed, and Stephanie crouched low to bestow a hug. 'Be a good girl for Sarah. Love you.'

'Yes. Love you, too,' Emma responded, tightening her arms around her mother's neck for a long minute.

Special, Stephanie accorded silently. The love of a child was unconditional, and therefore something to treasure.

'Okay,' she issued as she kissed her daughter's cheek and broke contact. 'Time to go.'

She could handle the daily routine of leaving Emma in care, for there was no other option. However, leaving her at night proved a wrench every time, no matter how she rationalized that she only socialized when the job demanded it.

Tonight's soiree was being held in a penthouse apartment situated opposite the Sheraton Mirage to celebrate soaring sales of an imported line of luxury lingerie. Successful advertising, publicity, promotion and marketing had attracted the eye of the Gold Coast's glitterati, resulting in a runaway success. The firm's European director had opted to fly in from Milan to inspect the firm's first Australian boutique and, rumor had it, to inspect his recently acquired apartment in the luxurious Palazzo Versace.

Stephanie reached Main Beach at six-thirty, parked in the underground car park beneath the complex, then rode the lift to the main foyer. Directions to the designated penthouse were easy to follow, and minutes later she'd cleared security and was led by a hostess into a large formal entertaining area filled with mingling guests.

A waiter appeared almost instantly and proffered a tray containing a selection of hors d'oeuvres. They were bite-size, and Stephanie took one, then at the waiter's encouragement, she selected another. There was champagne, which she declined in favor of flavored mineral water.

'Isn't this something else?'

She turned at the sound of a familiar voice, and offered the advertising executive a warm smile. 'Something,' she agreed, following his gaze as it encompassed the luxurious furnishings, magnificent tiling, the expensive paintings adorning the wall, each of which appeared to be genuine originals.

The million-dollar view out over the Broadwater, the many high-rise apartment buildings to the hills in the distance was picture-perfect by daylight. In another hour, when darkness fell, it would provide a fairyland of light against the backdrop of an indigo sky.

'It would appear lingerie does very well.'

'It's high-quality luxury, exceptional workmanship,' Stephanie stated, and incurred a slightly cynical smile.

'And ruinously expensive.'

'It has the name,' she said simply.

'Which we help promote.'

She inclined her head. 'Successfully.' Her gaze skimmed the room, touching on the occasional familiar face. A waiter proffered a tray of savories, and she accepted one, aware of hunger pangs and the knowledge she wouldn't eat dinner.

'If you'll excuse me,' she indicated minutes later. 'There's someone I want to talk to.'

During the next hour she mixed and mingled with fellow guests, some of whom she knew, others who clearly represented the cream of Gold Coast society.

Their host was a charming Italian whose attractive good looks caused more than one female heart to flutter in anticipation of gaining his attention.

Stephanie found it mildly amusing to observe the subtle, and not so subtle, attempts to flirt and charm him into more than a fleeting conversation. Some of it was merely harmless game-playing, which he dealt with the ease of long practice.

Anytime soon an announcement would be made, the host would deliver a gratifying speech, there would be the obligatory champagne toast, coffee would be offered, then she could leave and drive home.

Her gaze shifted, made restless by some indefinable shift in the room's occupants. Her skin's surface contracted in an involuntary shiver, almost a gesture of self-defense, and a slight frown creased her forehead. What on earth…

Then she glimpsed a tall broad-shouldered frame, and the breath caught in her throat at the sight of a familiar dark well-groomed head.

It couldn't be…could it? Her attention was riveted

as she watched the man turn toward her, and had her worst fears confirmed.

Raoul Lanier.

His features were unmistakable. The sculpted bone structure, broad cheekbones, the slant of his jaw, the wide set of those dark gray eyes. And the mouth.

Her eyes honed on that sensuously curved mouth, and remembered how it felt to have it close over her own. A slight tremor shook her slender frame, and she controlled it, barely.

With a sense of mesmerized fascination she watched as he paused to utter a few words to the person he was speaking to, then he turned and began making his way toward her.

For one wild moment she considered leaving. And she almost did, except instinct warned he would probably follow.

As he drew close she ignored her body's reaction and consciously took a slow steadying breath, aware the room and its occupants faded into obscurity.

There was only him, and an acute awareness she was loath to acknowledge.

'Stephanie.'

'Don't tell me,' she began in a voice edged with cynicism. 'Our host is a friend of yours.'

Raoul's eyes assumed a musing gleam. 'We attended the same university.'

'Sheer coincidence, of course,' she continued wryly. 'That you both happen to be in Australia at the same time. Staying not only in the same state, but the same city.'

He inclined his head, and moved in close to make room for a guest intent on beckoning the waiter.

Their bodies almost touched, and she instinctively moved back a pace.

Had he known she'd be here? 'I wouldn't have thought feminine lingerie would interest you.' She'd meant it to be a cutting remark, but as soon as the words were out of her mouth she realized their implication.

'It depends on the woman,' he intoned with dry amusement. 'And whether I'm sufficiently fascinated to want to remove it.'

The very thought of those clever hands easing a bra strap off a smooth shoulder, fingers skillfully manipulating a clasp, then lingering at the curve of a feminine waist before sliding lacy briefs down over slender hips...

Stop it. Wayward thoughts and a vivid imagination could only spell trouble.

'If you'll excuse me,' Stephanie said firmly, intending to remove herself as far away as possible from this disturbing man.

'No.'

She looked at him in silent askance, unaware that her eyes deepened in color and assumed a warning sparkle. 'What do you mean—*no?*'

His fingers closed over her elbow. 'Let me introduce you to Bruno.'

She shot him a fulminating glare. 'Get your hand off me.'

'*Merde,*' he swore softly. 'You try my patience.'

'Should I offer to mediate?' an amused male voice intruded.

Stephanie turned and came face to face with her host. A man whose eyes held wisdom and astute knowledge.

'Are you not going to introduce me to this young lady?'

'Bruno Farelli,' Raoul indicated smoothly. 'Stephanie Sommers.'

Bruno took her hand in his and lifted it to his lips. 'Stephanie,' he acknowledged. 'A pleasure.' His dark eyes gleamed with latent humor as he indicated Raoul. 'You do not like this man?'

'He irritates the hell out of me.'

Bruno's amusement was barely restrained. 'Interesting. Women usually fall at his feet.'

'How—' she paused deliberately, then continued with pseudo sweetness '—foolish of them.'

'Raoul must bring you to dinner,' Bruno drawled. 'My wife will enjoy your company.'

'I don't think—'

'Adriana was unable to join me tonight. My daughter did not travel well on the long flight.'

'I'm sorry,' Stephanie said with genuine sympathy.

He regarded her for several long seconds. 'Yes, I do believe you are,' he accorded quietly, pausing as his personal assistant drew close and murmured a brief message. Bruno nodded, then cast Stephanie and Raoul an apologetic glance. 'We will talk later. Now I must say a few words to my guests.'

The words were practiced, but sincere, and the

small surprise was a sneak preview of next season's new lingerie designs, which three models displayed to perfection. Expertly choreographed, the brief parade provided a tantalizing glimpse of what would appear in the boutique a few months from now.

It was a masterly stroke, and a successful one, judging by the buzz of voiced approval. Many of the women would purchase to titillate their husbands, whilst some of the men would designate a gift to a mistress, Stephanie deduced with a degree of cynicism.

'Can I get you another drink?'

Her glass was almost empty, and she surveyed it speculatively, not wanting to offer any encouragement for Raoul to remain at her side. 'I think I'll wait for coffee.'

'Which probably won't be served for another half hour,' Raoul drawled, and she offered him a witching smile that didn't reach her eyes.

'Then you mustn't let me keep you.'

Amusement tinged his expression. 'A politely veiled directive?'

'However did you guess?'

He was silent for several seconds, then he ventured with dangerous softness, 'Did Emma's father hurt you so badly?'

She met his gaze with fearless disregard, aware he saw more than she wanted anyone to see. It unsettled her, and attacked the carefully constructed wall she'd erected guarding her emotions.

A mix of emotions warred with each other as she

sought to control them. 'It's none of your business,' she managed to say with equal quietness.

There was a ruthlessness evident in those compelling features she found disconcerting.

'Does it not occur to you that I might choose to make it my business?'

'And if I choose not to let you?'

He was silent for several long seconds. 'Do you think you can stop me?'

She deliberately raked him from head to toe, and back again. 'You'd be a fool to even try.'

'I've been accorded many things,' Raoul said with indolent amusement. 'A fool isn't one of them.'

She'd had enough. Enough of this indomitable man, the party, and she wanted nothing more than to leave. Except her boss would undoubtedly frown on her early departure.

'Excuse me,' she voiced coolly. 'There are a few business associates I really should speak to.'

He let her go, watching as she eased her way across the room, pausing to chat momentarily before moving on. She possessed a natural grace, a fluidity of movement that reminded him of a dancer on stage.

'Lovely evening,' a pleasant feminine voice intruded, and he shifted his attention to the strikingly beautiful young blonde at his side, who, he acknowledged cynically, was aware of every feminine ploy and not averse to using each and every one of them.

Her conversation was scintillating with just the right degree of sexual promise in the full mouth, the touch of her hand on his arm.

Yet she didn't interest him, and all too frequently he found his attention straying to an attractive blue-eyed strawberry blonde who was as intent on fighting the sexual tension between them as he was in pursuing it.

Stephanie sipped the contents of her glass and fought the temptation to check her watch.

'All alone?'

Her heart sank a little as she summoned a polite smile.

'Samuel,' she acknowledged. As an advertising executive, Samuel Stone was almost without equal. As a man, he possessed one fatal flaw: he believed he was God's gift to women.

'You *have* moved in exalted circles tonight. The elder Lanier brother, and none other than Bruno Farelli himself paying you attention.' He moved close and ran an idle finger down the length of her arm. 'Nice going, darling. I wonder who you'll choose.'

'Neither.'

'Thus leaving the coast clear for me?'

Stephanie swept him a cool glance. 'When are you going to stop playing this wearisome game?'

His smile held a slightly cruel twist. 'You're the one I haven't caught, Stephanie.'

'You never will,' she stated dryly.

'Never is a long time, darling, and I'm remarkably persistent.'

'Two years, and you still haven't got the message.' She shot him an exasperated look. 'How many times do I need to spell it out?'

'You do disinterest well.'

This was becoming tiresome. 'It's for real, Samuel.'

'Why don't I believe you?'

'Because you have a serious ego problem.' She caught sight of two waiters setting up urns, cups and saucers. Thank heavens!

'Come out with me afterward. We'll go on to a nightclub, dance a little, get comfortable...'

'No.' She turned away from him only to have his hand take possession of hers. 'Don't do this, Samuel,' she warned in a deadly quiet voice.

'I believe the lady said no,' a faintly accented voice stated with dangerous silkiness.

Oh Lord, this was just what she needed. Two men at daggers drawn in a bid for her attention. She should have been flattered. Instead she felt vaguely sickened.

'I was hoping to change her mind,' Samuel indicated, releasing her hand.

Raoul's gaze was intent. 'I would say your luck just ran out.'

Samuel inclined his head in an elaborate bow. 'See you around, Stephanie.'

Not if I see you first, she vowed silently.

'You work with him?' Raoul queried when Samuel was out of earshot.

'Liaise,' Stephanie enlightened. 'Advertising and marketing go hand-in-hand.' She drew a deep breath and released it slowly. 'If you'll excuse me, I'll go get some coffee.'

'I'll join you.'

She gave him a sharp look, opened her mouth to decline his company, then closed it again.

'Emma has fully recovered?'

'Yes.' She was conscious of being unobtrusively led toward the table where coffee and tea were being dispensed. 'Yes, she has.'

'Two coffees. One black, the other white with one sugar,' Raoul instructed, then with a cup held in each hand he indicated the wide expanse of floor-to-ceiling glass. 'Let's go take a look at the view.'

Darkness had descended, and the many high-rise buildings appeared as brightly lit towers set against an inky sky. There were boats anchored in the vast marina, and the water resembled dark satin ribboned by the reflection of an ascending moon.

Stephanie stood in silence and sipped her coffee, increasingly aware of Raoul's close proximity as she focused on the immediately adjoining restaurant complex. Patrons enjoying their meal were partly visible, and there were couples, families, strolling along the boardwalk, pausing from time to time to admire some of the large cabin cruisers moored side by side.

It was a peaceful sight, with the sound of music providing a background to the chatter and laughter.

A powerful engine sprang to life from the marina, and minutes later a fully lit cruiser eased out from its berth and headed toward the main channel.

'This reminds me a little of the south of France,' Raoul revealed, indicating the marina. 'Have you traveled at all?'

'North America.' It seemed ages ago, a part of her past she no longer chose to dwell on.

'A holiday?'

'Yes.' A conducted tour in the company of the man she was to marry. Post Ben, pre-Emma.

'You visited New York?'

'I loved the beat of the city, the pulse of life. Seen as a tourist,' she ventured quietly. 'I imagine everyday reality causes it to lose some of the glamour.'

She finished the last of her coffee. 'I really must leave. Sarah has exams tomorrow, and I promised not to be late.'

'I'll walk you to your car.'

'There's no need. I parked in the Mirage shopping complex, and the area is well-lit.'

'Come, we'll find Bruno and you can tell him you've enjoyed a pleasant evening.'

'I can do that quite well on my own.'

He took her cup and placed it down onto a nearby side table along with his own.

'You don't listen, do you?' Stephanie vented with angry resignation as he accompanied her across the room.

Bruno was engaged in conversation with two men, and he looked up as Raoul drew close.

'You are leaving? So soon?'

'It's been a lovely evening,' Stephanie complimented with a warm smile. 'Thank you.'

'I will be in touch with Raoul about dinner. Toward the end of the week?'

'I don't think—'

'We'll confirm with you,' Raoul indicated smoothly.

Stephanie waited until they gained the main foyer before trusting herself to speak. 'Just what did you think you were doing back there?'

'Specifically?'

'Accepting a dinner invitation on my behalf!'

'My exact words conveyed we'd confirm.'

She shot him a baleful glare as they passed through the front entrance. *'We?'* Her voice rose a fraction. *'You* can make whatever plans you like!'

'I intend to. Be aware they'll also include you.'

'The hell they will!' They gained the pavement, and she turned to face him, anger emanating from every pore. 'I don't need a bodyguard, and I especially don't need you to assume a role in my life.' She undid the clasp of her evening purse and extracted her car keys. 'Good night!'

She'd parked the car at street level, and there was only a short distance to walk. She gained less than half a dozen paces when Raoul fell into step at her side.

'You are, without doubt, the most infuriating man I've ever had the misfortune to meet!' she vented furiously as she reached her car.

'In that case, I have nothing to lose.' In a swift synchronized movement he brought her close, slid one hand to cup her head as he captured her lips with his own.

For several long seconds she fought against succumbing to the melting sensation threatening to destroy all rational thought. Her hands lifted to pummel his shoulders, only to fall onto each forearm as she opened her mouth to him.

Oh God, she begged in silent plea as his tongue took an evocative exploratory sweep. Don't do this to me. Why, *why* were her emotions at such variance with the dictates of her brain? All it took was his touch, and she fell to pieces.

Raoul sensed the moment she gave in, and he deepened the kiss, taking her to new heights in emotional intensity.

Her response drove him to cup her bottom and lift her close against him. He wanted more, much more, and the temptation to invite her to his hotel suite was imperative. Except such an action would destroy any advantage he might already have gained.

Instead he eased the pressure, lightening the kiss until his lips brushed gently back and forth over her own, and he slid his hands to cradle her face as he slowly lifted his head.

Her eyes were wide, dilated, and filled with shimmering moisture. The sight of those unspilled tears caused his gut to tighten, and undid him more than any words she might have uttered.

He brushed his thumb over the lower curve of her lip, and felt its faint tremor. He wanted to draw her back into his arms, and simply hold her. Rarely had he glimpsed such naked vulnerability in a woman's eyes, and there was a part of him that seethed in silent anger against the man who had put it there.

He saw the effort it cost her to regain control, to gather her defenses together and step back from him.

His hands slid down her arms and settled on her wrists. 'Stephanie—'

'I have to go. Please.'

The last word held a slightly desperate edge, and he released her, took the keys from her nerveless fingers, unlocked the car door and saw her seated behind the wheel.

Stephanie fired the engine, then barely resisted the temptation to reverse at speed, then send the car tearing out onto the road.

It was only supreme control that stopped her, and she didn't cast Raoul so much as a glance as she eased into the flow of traffic.

She wasn't conscious of having held her breath until she released it in a long pent-up groan. *Why* had she allowed herself to fall into that kiss?

A choked laugh caught in her throat. Raoul Lanier hadn't really given her an option! Except she hadn't fought him, and she should have. For her own emotional sanity, not to mention her peace of mind.

She drove automatically, conscious of the traffic, the intersections, the computerized lights as she traversed the main highway toward Mermaid Beach.

Yet she retained a vivid image of how Raoul's mouth had possessed her own, the slide of his hands, and her body's damnable reaction.

She had sworn after Ben that she'd never allow another man to get close to her again. She'd trusted one, and had that trust broken. Just as she had loved, and discovered her interpretation of *love* and Ben's didn't match.

There was Emma, dear sweet innocent Emma. It was enough. She didn't want or need a man to complicate her life. And she especially didn't need Raoul Lanier, who, in a week or two, would board a plane and jet off to the other side of the world to take up where he left off with his life.

He probably had a mistress.

Now why did that cause her stomach to perform a painful somersault? She didn't *like* the man, she definitely disliked the way he affected her, and she had no intention of allowing a personal relationship to develop between them.

Stephanie reached the fringes of suburban Mermaid Beach, and minutes later she turned into her driveway, activated a modem and garaged the car.

Indoors, Sarah relayed all was well and gathered up her books, then Stephanie kept watch until the girl reached her home safely before locking up.

Emma slept peacefully, and Stephanie tucked in the blanket, moved the teddy bear, then quietly retreated to her own room.

CHAPTER FIVE

IT HADN'T been the best of mornings, Stephanie reflected as she checked her computer's electronic mail. No doubt compounded by the fact she hadn't slept well and was nursing a headache.

One message was headlined as Urgent, and she uttered a soft curse as she clicked it open. The date for the movie's photographic shoot needed to be rescheduled. Could she contact the Sheraton management, organize a suitable time to check the proposed layout, liaise with the photographer and confirm this afternoon?

She reached for her phone, only to have it beep, and she automatically lifted the receiver. 'Yes?'

'I have Raoul Lanier on hold,' Isabel intoned.

Stephanie's stomach immediately curled into a tight ball. 'Have him call back.'

'Okay. Any message?'

Not one you could repeat, she ruminated darkly. 'No,' she managed to say evenly. 'Can you get me Alex Stanford on the line? Try his cell phone.' The photographer was one of the best, and with luck he'd be able to spare half an hour to go over the proposed shots.

Thirty minutes later she'd tied it all together, and

ignoring her scheduled lunch break she slid into her car and drove to Main Beach and the Sheraton Hotel.

Alex was waiting in the lobby when she arrived, and together they descended the central staircase, walked out to the pool area, tossed around indoor and outdoor locations, the portrayed mood she wanted to convey, and fixed on a few possible time frames for the following week, subject to confirmation.

Stephanie extracted her diary, wrote in the dates and times, noted contact names at the film studio, advertising, wardrobe.

'Okay, that's it,' she assured, replacing the diary into her satchel. 'I'll ring when I've pinned it down. Thanks,' she added with a genuine smile as they reentered the lobby. 'I appreciate your help.' Her cell phone rang, and she wriggled her fingers at Alex as he departed for the lift, then she took the call.

Five minutes later she pushed the cell phone into her bag and made for the central stairs leading up to reception. Her stomach grumbled, reminding her she'd had to forego lunch, and she contemplated whether to cross the footbridge to the shopping complex for a coffee and sandwich, or whether she'd simply stop somewhere and pick up something to eat on the way back to the office.

She reached the top of the stairs and made her way through the foyer. Coffee and a sandwich in a café overlooking the Broadwater won out.

'Stephanie.'

It was an instantly recognizable male voice, the

drawling faintly accented tone causing all her fine body hairs to stand up in protective self-defense as she turned to face the man who had indirectly caused her a sleepless night.

Raoul Lanier. Looking every inch the powerful executive, attired in a dark business suit, crisp white shirt and dark silk tie. Expensive tailoring emphasized his breadth of shoulder, accentuated his height and added to an overall aura of sophistication.

She looked…fragile, Raoul decided as he subjected her to a studied appraisal. Her eyes were the deepest blue, and there were faint shadows apparent that indicated she hadn't enjoyed a peaceful night's sleep…any more than he had. Something that pleased him.

Stephanie saw that he wasn't alone. Bruno Farelli, an attractive blonde, and a young child were with him.

Her cool gaze was controlled, her slight smile a mere facsimile. 'Raoul, Bruno,' she acknowledged.

'A pleasure to see you again,' Bruno enthused, and indicated the woman at his side. 'Allow me to introduce my wife, Adriana, and our daughter, Lucia.'

The little girl stole her heart, she resembled a miniature angel, beautifully dressed with gorgeous blond curly hair and a winsome smile.

'Adriana.' Stephanie's features softened as she greeted the child. 'Hello, Lucia.'

'Bruno mentioned you,' Adriana offered warmly. 'We have just emerged from a long lunch.'

Stephanie responded an appropriate platitude. 'I hope you enjoy your stay here.'

'You must join us for dinner,' Adriana pressed with a smile. 'I believe you have a little girl of Lucia's age. It would be delightful for them to meet. Are you free tomorrow evening?'

Oh hell. How did she handle that? With grace, she decided reluctantly. Bruno Farelli was a very influential man, and the agency she worked for was handling his account. To refuse would not only be impolite, but a bad move, professionally. She could only hope Raoul Lanier wasn't included in the invitation.

'Thank you, I'd like that.'

'Shall we say six, at our apartment?'

Her cell phone rang, and she reached for it, ascertained the combination of digits displayed in the window, and offered an apologetic smile. 'I'm sorry, I'll have to take this. If you'll excuse me?' She focused her attention on Adriana. 'Six, tomorrow evening. I'll look forward to it.' She inclined her head briefly, then she turned and activated the call as she made her way toward the main entrance.

Definitely a latte and sandwich, she decided minutes later, and she ordered, then ate beneath a shade umbrella, opting to check Bruno's lingerie boutique window display whilst in the shopping complex.

It was almost three when she entered the office, and what remained of the afternoon was caught up with numerous phone calls together with the completion of a lengthy report.

Consequently it was well after five when she collected Emma from the day care center, and the headache that had bothered her most of the day developed sufficiently to warrant medication.

At eight, with Emma safely asleep, she took a leisurely shower, luxuriating in the relaxing jet of warm water as it soothed the kinks from her neck. Rose-scented soap left her skin silky smooth and exuding a delicate fragrance. Toweled dry she added matching dusting powder and pulled on a freshly laundered T-shirt.

Not exactly an ultrafeminine image, she mentally derided as she caught a glance of her mirrored reflection. Not that it mattered one little bit, for there was no man in her life to tease and tantalize with silk and lace.

Nor did she want one, she silently assured as she applied a thin film of night cream to her face, smoothed the excess onto her hands, then switched off the light and crept into bed.

So why did she lay awake haunted by one man's profile? And have her thoughts stray as she imagined how his skin would feel beneath her touch? Would his muscles flex as he sought control? And at what point would he lose it?

He had the look, the touch, she acknowledged, that promised unbridled primitive passion. The skill and intimate knowledge to drive a woman wild.

Thinking just *how* wild was an infinitely dangerous exercise, for it brought a vivid reminder of her relationship with Ben...a man who had taken his pleasure without consideration for her own. And she, through reticence and naiveté, had enjoyed the closeness and warmth, while longing for more.

Blind trust and immature love, she acknowledged with innate honesty. Had she been older, wiser, in the ways of men, she'd have seen the weakness, the selfishness for what it was. Instead she had made excuses for him and blamed herself for his shortcomings.

Fool. How long before she would have seen him for what he was? Her pregnancy had been an act of God...and a gastro bug, which destroyed the contraceptive pill's effectiveness at the most crucial part of her cycle.

Emma, dear sweet Emma. Ben's reaction had been so abhorrent, from that moment Emma had become *hers,* solely hers.

With a determination Stephanie barely recognized in herself, she'd left Sydney, family and friends, and relocated to the Gold Coast, carving a niche for herself at what she did best...marketing. She'd worked up until two weeks before Emma's birth, taken a month's maternity leave, then returned to the workforce.

Her mother visited twice a year, and took Emma back to Sydney for a few weeks, and Stephanie returned there for her annual holidays.

For almost four years she'd been happy and content with her life. Until now, when Raoul Lanier had appeared on the scene, disrupting her carefully chosen lifestyle, attacking her libido, and causing her to long for something that could only bring grief.

The only way out was not to see him again. A silent bubble of laughter rose and died in her throat. How did she do that, when he had involved himself in one of her work assignments? Everywhere she went, he seemed to be *there*. Legitimately, she had to concede.

She closed her eyes then opened them again to stare into the room's darkness.

A week or two, then he'd be gone. Surely she could survive that length of time?

The shrill peal of the phone jerked her instantly into a sitting position, and she reached for the bedside lamp with one hand and the extension receiver with the other.

Her voice was breathless, startled, apprehensive, and she inwardly cursed herself as she checked the time.

'Did I wake you?' Raoul's voice was deep, and vaguely husky.

She wasn't conscious of holding her breath, until it released in a rush. 'No.' She clutched the receiver, and mentally counted to three. 'No, you didn't. What do you want?'

'You neglected to return my call.'

'I wasn't aware it was necessary,' she said coolly. 'Besides, I understand my secretary asked you to call back.'

'I didn't have the opportunity until now.'

'It couldn't wait until tomorrow?'

'Michel requests you fax him an update on estimated marketing and advertising expenses. He wants to check them against the preliminary figures. Have you a pen and paper handy? I'll give you his e-mail address.'

'Just a minute.' She opened the pedestal drawer and extracted a pad and pen. 'Okay, what is it?' She wrote it down, then repeated it. 'I'll get on to it first thing in the morning.'

'There is just one more thing,' he drawled.

'And that is?'

'I'll collect you and Emma at five forty-five tomorrow evening.'

She closed her eyes and opened them again. Why, for one minute, had she thought he might not be included in Bruno's invitation? 'No. I'll drive to the hotel.'

'*Sacré bleu*, why must you be so independent?'

'You're already staying at the Sheraton,' she stated with cool logic. 'Why collect me?'

'You would prefer to drive home at night to an empty house with a young child in your care?'

This was too much. *He* was too much! 'I would *prefer* it if you weren't there at all tomorrow night,' she flung angrily.

'My presence unsettles you?' Raoul pursued with mocking amusement.

'You flatter yourself,' she said icily. 'If there's nothing else you need to discuss, I'd like to go back to bed. And in future,' she added for good measure, 'please keep business calls to business hours.'

He laughed, a deep-throated chuckle that incensed her to such a degree she hung up on him.

Insufferable man. She thumped her pillow, snapped off the light, then pulled up the covers and settled down to sleep.

Except sleep was never more distant, and she cursed him to hell and back as the dark hours crept slowly to midnight and beyond.

The insistent peal of the alarm clock brought her sharply awake, and she depressed the button before slipping wearily from the bed.

Feed and dress Emma, feed the cat, take out the trash, make coffee, eat, pack Emma's lunch and fill drink bottles ready for day care...

Stephanie went through the motions automatically, completed essential household chores, then she dressed for work, delivered Emma to the day care center and drove in to the office.

It proved to be a day where anything that could go wrong, did. She needed every organizational skill she possessed to arrange the smooth transition from delivery of stock to television promotion. A company drivers' strike provided a delay while she arranged alternate mode of transport. Wardrobe didn't supply the right size or the right color for the model promoting the product. Phone calls weren't returned, and she had to chase up advertising.

When she left the office at five all she wanted to do was collect Emma, go home, relax and unwind.

Instead she needed to bathe and dress her daughter, grab a quick shower, throw on some clothes, apply makeup…all in the space of twenty-five minutes.

There was a part of her that wanted to ring and cancel, except that would amount to a cop-out, and she was damned if she'd allow Raoul Lanier the satisfaction. She'd attend, and enjoy herself. For Emma's sake, and that of her hosts. The indomitable Frenchman could, she decided, go *jump* for all she cared.

It was nothing short of a miracle that she was ready on time. Elegant evening trousers with matching camisole in a deep ultraviolet highlighted her cream textured skin and emphasized her eyes. Emma wore a pale blue print dress with white shoes and socks. Her very best outfit, Stephanie mused, taking pleasure in her daughter's delightful anticipation of the evening ahead.

From a personal aspect, she hadn't had the opportunity to give it more than a passing thought. Now that they were on the verge of leaving, the prospect of spending yet another few hours in Raoul Lanier's company bothered her more than she wanted to admit.

'Okay, sweetheart,' she said gently as she collected her keys and evening purse. 'Let's go.'

They made it to the front door, only to have the bell peal as Stephanie reached to open it, and her heart raced into overdrive at the sight of Raoul Lanier standing on the porch.

'You shouldn't have come,' she said at once, doing her best to remain polite in Emma's presence.

He spared her a long hard glance. 'I said I would collect you.'

He was angry, she could tell from the set of his jaw, the slight thickening of his accent. It was becoming a battle of wills—*hers, his*—and for some reason, despite her determination, she felt she was treading shaky ground.

Raoul turned to greet Emma, who, an innocent traitor, appeared delighted not only to see him, but excited at the prospect of being driven in a different car.

A large late-model sedan, Stephanie saw at once. 'I'll need to get Emma's booster seat,' she indicated, and crossed to the garage. 'She's under the legal age to be able to travel without it.' One of the reasons I would have preferred to use my own car, she added silently, then caught Raoul's perceptive look, and knew he wasn't fooled in the slightest.

Three more minutes, and their cars would have passed in the street. He wanted to shake her. Independence in a woman was a fine thing, but this particular young woman was intent on carrying it too far.

Raoul drove with care, traversing the northbound highway with the ease of a man well used to handling both left- and right-hand drive.

Emma's excited childish chatter precluded the need to search for conversation, and Stephanie experienced a mixture of apprehension and trepidation as Raoul swept the car into the underground parking lot beneath the Palazzo Versace.

Save your nerves for a few hours' time when you leave, she admonished silently. Although with luck, Raoul would indulge in a few glasses of wine during dinner, and she could insist on taking a taxi home.

Two hours, three at the most, then she could leave, social obligation complete, and thereafter contact with Bruno Farelli would be restricted to office hours and confined to business matters.

Some hope, she realized with a sinking heart, as the evening progressed. *Luck* wasn't on her side, in any respect.

Emma and Lucia, with the natural instinct of children, bonded immediately. To the extent it seemed as if they'd known each other from the cradle.

Adriana's warmth and sparkling humor made it impossible to retain a polite distance. Both she and Bruno were friendly convivial hosts who went to great pains to ensure Stephanie felt at ease.

They would have succeeded handsomely if it hadn't been for Raoul's presence. For it was *he* who set her nerves on edge. He who caused her heart to beat faster as she forced herself to sample the various courses, sip a little wine, and converse with apparent ease.

Did any one of them realize just how tense she was beneath the relaxed facade? Could anyone detect the way her pulse thudded at the base of her throat? Or how her body tingled with electrifying awareness because of the man seated at her side?

The food was superb, she was certain of it, except her taste buds appeared to have gone on strike.

This was madness. A divine insanity that had no base in her reality.

How long before she could escape? There was dessert still to come, followed by coffee. Another hour?

'Which theme park would you recommend for Lucia's benefit?' Adriana queried. 'We are only on the Coast for such a short time.'

'Dreamworld is wonderful,' Stephanie answered automatically. 'And Seaworld. Each have various rides and attractions. I've taken Emma to both, and while she enjoyed Seaworld, Dreamworld was her favorite.'

'Bruno has Saturday free. We'd love you and Emma to join us. The girls get on well together, and it would be so nice for Lucia to have Emma's company.'

'Dreamworld,' Emma parroted with excitement. 'Please, Mommy.'

'*Si,*' Lucia echoed. 'Dreamworld.'

'English, Lucia,' Adriana admonished gently.

'Perhaps Stephanie already has plans for the weekend,' Raoul indicated, offering her a silent challenge to refuse.

'Saturday is fine,' Stephanie answered evenly in a determined effort to prove she wouldn't rise to his bait. 'Thank you. We'd be delighted to join you.'

Adriana looked pleased as she stood and gathered up the dinner plates. 'I'll get dessert. I hope you like tiramisu?'

'Love it,' Stephanie assured. 'Can I help with anything?'

'You're very kind, but everything is organized.'

Coffee followed the superb dessert, and it was almost nine when Stephanie indicated she must leave.

'It's been a lovely evening,' she said warmly, extending her thanks. 'I'll look forward to Saturday.' She meant it, for Adriana was delightful, and Emma would love sharing the adventures of Dreamworld with Lucia.

'Let me have your telephone number.' Adriana beckoned for her to cross to an escritoire, where she extracted pen and paper. 'I'll ring and arrange a time to meet.'

Stephanie withdrew her cell phone. 'I'll call a taxi.'

Adriana gave her a thoughtful glance, and opted to remain quiet.

A few minutes, the dispatcher relayed, as a taxi had just dropped someone off at the Sheraton.

Collecting Emma, bidding her hosts good-night, was achieved in minimum time.

'Cancel the taxi,' Raoul instructed with deadly quiet as they made their way toward the lift.

'No.'

His expression hardened, and his eyes resembled dark gray slate. 'Cancel, Stephanie,' he voiced quietly. 'Or I will.'

She shot him a cool glare, which changed to scandalized surprise as he calmly took the cell phone from her hand, pressed Redial, and canceled the taxi.

She badly wanted to tell him to go take a flying

leap, except such behavior would only startle Emma. It would have to wait, she decided vengefully, until they were alone.

Stephanie was supremely conscious of him as they rode the lift down to the car park, and it took every reserve of strength not to wrench Emma from his arms.

Who did he think he was, invading her life, taking charge, issuing orders? It was a wonder steam wasn't escaping from her ears as she banked down her anger.

Fortunately Emma's excitement resulted in practically nonstop chatter during the fifteen-minute drive to Mermaid Beach, which meant Stephanie was able to respond to her daughter and totally ignore the man behind the wheel of the car.

The instant Raoul pulled into her driveway she undid her seat belt, and no sooner had he brought the car to a halt that she slid from the passenger seat in a bid to extricate Emma as quickly as possible.

'There's no need for you to get out,' Stephanie said tightly as he copied her actions. 'I can manage.'

'I am sure you can,' he evinced silkily as he crossed to her side. 'Let me take Emma.'

She didn't want him in the house. 'No. I'm fine. Say good-night, darling,' she bade Emma seconds later, only to give a startled gasp as Raoul removed the keys from her fingers and pushed one into the lock of the front door.

Naturally he got it right the first time, and she

clenched her teeth in exasperation as he followed her indoors.

Stephanie threw him a look that should have felled him. 'I'd like you to leave. Now.'

'Put Emma to bed, Stephanie,' Raoul drawled in a deceptively silky voice. He smiled at the little girl nestled in her mother's arms. 'Good night, poppet. Sweet dreams.'

'Kiss good night,' Emma said with unblinking solemnity, and held out her arms.

Raoul leaned forward and brushed a soft childish cheek with his lips, then watched as Stephanie turned away and moved down the hallway.

Did he have any idea what that gesture did to her? Almost before her eyes man and child were forming an affection that had no place to go. It wasn't fair to Emma, she decided as she undressed her daughter and went through the routine of getting her ready for bed.

It took a while for her to settle, given the excitement of the evening and the prospect of a visit to Dreamworld. But halfway through the usual nighttime story the long silky lashes began to droop as she drifted to sleep.

Stephanie waited a few minutes, then she adjusted the covers, turned down the light and gently closed the door as she left.

Raoul was in the lounge, one hand thrust into a trouser pocket, and he raked her slender form with compelling intensity as she crossed to stand behind a single chair.

'Don't presume to judge me by Emma's father.'

Her eyes flashed blue fire and her chin tilted as she threw him a venomous glare. 'You know nothing of Emma's father.'

'I know he holds no importance in your life.' He indicated the picture frames holding pride of place on the dropped table. 'There is no evidence of his existence.'

Anger flooded through her like an unstoppable tide, and the desire to shock caused a flow of words she had no intention of uttering.

'Ben is dead.'

If that stark announcement surprised him, he gave no evidence of it, and that infuriated her further.

'You want to know details?' she vented. 'We were childhood sweethearts who grew up together, fell in love and got engaged. Then I fell pregnant. A classic mistake caused by a low dosage pill and a gastric attack.' Her expression sobered, became shuttered as some of the pain returned.

'The man I thought I knew as well as I knew myself suggested I *take care of it* on the grounds a child would complicate our lives.' Her face paled at the memory of those ghastly arguments. 'I refused.' She felt her features tighten as scenes flashed through her mind. The anger, the stinging retribution. 'He opted out and took a flight to Canada, only to die a few months later in a skiing accident.'

She drew a deep calming breath, then released it, hating herself for the tirade, and hating him even more for goading her into it.

'You intend excluding all men from your life, because one man ran away from responsibility?'

She'd dealt with this four years ago. Dealt with the pain of rejection, the degree of guilt for Ben's death. She didn't want to revive the past, for she'd learned the hard way that it had no part in her future.

'I want you to leave.'

'Not yet.'

'Who do you think you are?' On impulse she picked up a nearby ornament and hurled it at him only to see him field and catch it.

The action horrified her, and she stared at him in stunned disbelief for several long seconds.

'Dammit! What do you want from me?' The query came out as a strangled whisper.

'The opportunity to prove I'm not Ben.' His voice was dangerously quiet, and she was unable to look away.

'To what end?' she demanded, sorely tried. 'You're on the Coast how long? A week, two at the most.' Her gaze pierced his. 'Then what? You move on, New York, Paris...wherever. I can qualify a pleasant sojourn, but what about Emma? How does she deal with someone who affords her affection, then leaves?'

'I want to be with you.'

His meaning was unmistakable. 'Are you suggesting we scratch an *itch?*'

Her scandalized expression amused him. 'When I take you to bed,' he vowed silkily, 'it won't be merely to *scratch an itch.*'

'No,' she denied heatedly. 'Because you won't get anywhere near my bed!'

Raoul regarded her silently for a few seconds. 'You are so sure about that?'

She wasn't sure about anything where he was concerned. Already he'd managed to get beneath her skin, and that in itself was dangerous.

'Go find some other woman to fill your needs. I'm not into experimentation.'

'Neither am I,' Raoul assured pitilessly. 'And if I merely wanted a woman to *fill my needs,* why would I choose to continually do battle with *you?*'

'Because I make a change, and therefore present a challenge?'

'Is that what you think?'

'Damn you,' Stephanie snarled, almost at the end of her tether. 'What else is there for me to think?'

'You could try to trust me.'

'I trusted a man once,' she flung heatedly. 'Someone I'd known all my life. Why should I trust *you,* someone I've known for only a week!'

'Because I give my word that you can.'

'Words are easy,' she said bitterly.

She wasn't aware of him moving, yet he was close, much too close, and there was nothing she could do to escape his descending head as he claimed her mouth in a kiss that took her by complete surprise.

She expected force…a fierce unprincipled onslaught that was nothing less than an invasion.

Instead his touch was tactile, an evocative exploration that was incredibly gentle. Bewitching, enticing, it mesmerized her with a magic all its own, hinting at hunger and passion withheld.

Heat coursed through her veins, arousing acute sensuality, and her body swayed into his, craving closer contact as her arms slid up his shoulders and clung.

Raoul deepened the kiss, slowly and with infinite care, eliciting a response that drove him to the brink.

This wasn't the time, or the place, and he gradually withdrew, lightly brushing her lips with his own until they sought and rested against her temple.

How long they stood like that she wasn't sure. Long seconds, maybe minutes. Then he shifted a hand and cupped her chin, forcing her to meet his gaze.

'You want to deny *this?*' He cradled her face, and felt a tremor race through her body. 'Reject what we might have together?' He smoothed a thumb over her lips. 'I want you. For all the right reasons. I need you to want to take the first step.'

He lowered his head and kissed her, lightly teasing her tongue with his own, then he withdrew.

'I'm going to walk out the door. You have the number of my cell phone. If you don't ring me before I reach the hotel, I won't attempt to see you again.' He ran his thumb lightly over her lower lip, then pressed the pad against the slightly swollen center. 'Okay?'

'I don't want this,' she said in a desperate whisper.

'Wrong,' he denied gently. 'You don't want to be hurt.'

'That, too,' she admitted wretchedly, and he smiled.

'One day at a time, *cherie*, hmm?'

She wasn't capable of uttering a word.

He placed his hands over her own and gently disentangled them from his shoulders.

Her eyes clung to his, wide, dilated, unblinking as he stepped back a pace. She saw his lips curve into a faint smile that held quizzical warmth, and something else.

Then he turned and left the room. She heard the faint *snick* as the front door closed and the lock engaged, and seconds later his car engine purred into life, only to fade with distance.

Stephanie didn't move, she simply stared into space as she tried to collect her thoughts.

If she rang him, her life would never be the same. Yet if she didn't...would she live to regret not having taken that chance?

Life was all about chance. You could choose whether to welcome it with both hands. Or you could choose extreme caution, question every possibility, and never realize a dream.

What did she have to lose?

A hollow laugh rose and formed a lump in her throat. Oh *hell*. She was damned if she did, and damned if she didn't.

Impulse stirred her to action, and she extracted Raoul's business card, then made the call.

He picked up on the third ring. 'What took you so long?'

'A fight with my subconscious,' she answered honestly.

'*Merci.*'

His voice sounded deep and impossibly husky, and did strange things to her equilibrium.

'Good night.' She cut the connection, then stood in reflective silence.

What had she done? She was mad, *insane*. To contemplate aligning herself with someone of Raoul Lanier's caliber was akin to riding a tiger. But what a ride, a tiny imp taunted mercilessly.

Too restless to sleep, she retrieved fresh linen and made up the bed in the spare room ready for her mother. She also dusted, and put out fresh towels.

Then she made a cup of tea and flicked through the channels on cable television in the hope of finding something engrossing to watch, only to switch it off and pick up a book.

CHAPTER SIX

A *DELIVERY* of roses, a dozen beautiful pale pink buds sheathed in cellophane arrived in reception midafternoon, and Stephanie ignored her secretary's curiosity as she extracted the card.

Dinner tonight. Seven. Raoul.

'Shall I fetch a vase?'

She looked up at the sound of Isabel's voice. 'Thanks.'

'Your three-thirty appointment is waiting in reception. Shall I show her in?'

'Give me a few minutes, I need to make a call first.'

Seconds later she punched in a series of digits, and tried to calm her shredding nerves as she waited for Raoul to pick up.

A kiss didn't mean anything, despite the fact it was very skillfully executed and pushed all the right buttons, she conceded rationally, only to stifle a groan. Who did she think she was kidding?

'Lanier.'

His voice was deep, businesslike, and she forced herself to respond in kind. 'Stephanie.' She turned away from the desk and looked at the scene beyond the plate-glass window. 'Thank you for the roses.'

She felt like a gauche teenager, which was ridiculous!

'My pleasure.'

The husky faintly accented voice seeped into her body and curled around her nerve endings. She lifted a shaky hand and pushed back a stray tendril of hair.

It was crazy to feel so distracted, and her fingers tightened on the receiver as she sought composure. 'I can't make it tonight. My mother is arriving from Sydney on the evening flight.'

'You need to collect her from the airport.' He sounded vaguely amused, almost as if he *knew* the struggle she was having in order to remain calm.

'Yes. I'm sorry.'

'I'll look forward to meeting her—'

'Raoul—'

'When I collect you and Emma tomorrow,' he continued. 'Adriana mentioned meeting in the hotel foyer at nine-thirty.'

'It will be easier if I drive to the hotel.'

'We've been down this path before,' Raoul drawled. 'Nine-fifteen, Stephanie.'

'I don't like domineering men,' she retorted, and heard his soft husky laughter. Her voice assumed a definitive coolness. 'I have a client waiting.'

'Tomorrow, Stephanie,' he reminded a bare second before she disconnected the call.

'Nanna's coming, Nanna's coming. Big airplane,' Emma chanted on the way home, during her bath, over dinner and all the way down to Coolangatta airport.

'Nanna.' Stephanie had to physically restrain her from running to the entry doors the instant Emma caught sight of her grandmother walking the concourse.

'Celeste.' Stephanie greeted her mother with an affectionate hug, and took her carry-on bag so Celeste could gather Emma into her arms.

There wasn't a chance to get a word in edgeways as Emma excitedly regaled every detail about day care, her friends, the beach, the pool. Nonstop childish chatter ruled as Stephanie collected Celeste's bag from the luggage carousel.

'How are you, darling?' Celeste inquired of her daughter when there was a temporary lull.

'Fine,' Stephanie answered warmly. 'The job is going well.' She shot Celeste a quick smile. 'As you can see, Emma is great.'

'Dreamworld,' Emma chorused from the rear seat. 'Tomorrow me and Mommy and Lucia, and Raoul—' she struggled getting the name out '—are going to Dreamworld. Can Nanna come, too?'

'We'll talk about it later, sweetheart,' Celeste conceded.

It took a while for Emma to settle after they arrived home, and it was almost nine when Stephanie entered the lounge.

'I made some tea, darling.' Celeste indicated the sofa. 'Now come and sit down.'

'How is Dad?'

Celeste smiled warmly. 'Philip is fine. Still working too hard, but he enjoys the legal process, and criminal law is his life.'

It was lovely to catch up on all the news. Family comprised several cousins, aunts and uncles, her grandparents, and it was almost eleven when Celeste caught sight of the time.

'I think we should go to bed. We have plenty of time over the weekend to chat.'

'Would you like to come to Dreamworld with us tomorrow?' Stephanie asked as she straightened cushions and switched off the lamp.

'You're going with friends, aren't you, darling? I might just relax at home, and prepare a roast for dinner.'

Ever the mother, Stephanie conceded affectionately. Roast dinners, baking tins filled, extra for the freezer. She placed an arm around Celeste's waist as they traversed the short hallway. 'I've already washed curtains and bedspreads,' she warned with a smile. 'So don't even *think* about any spring-cleaning, okay?'

'I like to do things for you. I don't get the chance very often.'

Stephanie switched on the light in the spare bedroom. 'Sleep well, Celeste. I'll see you in the morning.'

A bright sunny day, with the promise of high temperatures, Stephanie saw as she opened shutters and let the light in.

It was early, only seven, but Emma had already stirred, and she popped an educational video into the VCR. 'Sit quietly,' she said. 'I'll get you some juice, then we'll have breakfast.'

Celeste joined them, and at eight-thirty Stephanie dressed Emma, packed a holdall with sunscreen cream, snacks, juice, bottled water, the utilitarian first-aid necessities and the seemingly hundred and one things needed when taking a child out for the day.

Then she quickly changed into stonewashed jeans and a blue singlet top, added a blouse, then tended to her makeup.

Emma had positioned herself on a chair beside the window overlooking the front driveway, and Stephanie heard her excited voice calling, 'Raoul's here. Raoul's here, Mommy.'

'There's no such thing as a quiet arrival,' Stephanie said wryly as Celeste rose to her feet.

'Oh my,' Celeste murmured as Raoul entered the hallway.

Attired in casual dress jeans, a navy polo shirt and trainers—sunglasses pushed high—he resembled something out of the pages of a men's fashion magazine.

Stephanie performed introductions. 'My mother, Celeste Sommers. Raoul Lanier.'

'A pleasure,' Raoul inclined, and Stephanie could almost sense his effect on her mother.

'Raoul, Raoul.' Emma launched herself at him, and he caught and lifted her high against his chest.

'*Bon jour,* Emma,' he greeted solemnly.

'Dreamworld. Got a cap.' She put a hand over the cap pulled down over her hair. 'Can we go?' She turned to her grandmother. 'Bye, Nanna.'

'Have a nice day,' Celeste said warmly.

Raoul took Emma to the car while Stephanie set the booster seat, and within minutes Raoul reversed down the driveway and headed toward the highway.

They entered the theme park shortly after ten, and both Emma and Lucia chattered with delight as the adults indulged them in a variety of rides and other features suitable for the very young.

Stephanie was supremely conscious of Raoul at her side, the light momentary brush of his hand at her waist, her shoulder. His smile did strange things to her composure, and her whole body seemed like a finely tuned instrument awaiting his touch.

It was madness, a madness she couldn't afford. For four years she'd marshaled her emotions and vowed never to allow another man to get beneath her skin. Now, no matter how hard she tried to avoid it, Raoul had skillfully managed to penetrate her defenses.

Could he sense her ambivalence? Probably, she perceived wryly. He seemed to have developed the uncanny knack of reading her mind, anticipating her thoughts.

Together with Bruno, Adriana and Lucia, they watched the tigers, rode the paddle steamer and witnessed the little girls' awe at the enacted mock train robbery.

There were several stops for liquid refreshment as

the day wore on, and after an alfresco lunch both little girls began to tire.

'I'll take her,' Raoul indicated when Stephanie lifted Emma into her arms, and as she was about to protest Emma leaned toward him with arms outstretched.

What could she say? To refuse would seem churlish. Besides, Emma was only copying Lucia, who was happily settled in the curve of her father's arm.

It didn't take long for two little heads to droop against two male shoulders, and Stephanie tried to ignore the sight of her daughter nestled comfortably in Raoul's arms. It looked natural, much too natural, and there was a part of her that wanted to tear Emma away.

Don't get too close. It's unfair, she longed to hurl at him. But with Bruno and Adriana within hearing distance, there wasn't much she could do except appear relaxed and at ease with the situation as they wandered in and out of several tourist and souvenir shops.

Lucia stirred a short while later, and almost on cue Emma lifted her head, focused on her surroundings and pointed to where several cartoon costumed characters were mingling among the crowd.

'Kenny Koala,' Emma chanted with renewed energy, and there were photographs taken with each costumed character, then after time-out for refreshments, they slowly made their way toward the main gate.

'It's been a lovely day.' Adriana leaned forward

and caught hold of Stephanie's hand. 'Thank you for bringing Emma. Lucia has had a wonderful time.'

'We've hired a cruiser and crew to tour the waterways tomorrow,' Bruno relayed as they reached their respective cars. 'We would like to have you join us.'

Raoul inclined his head. 'Stephanie?'

She'd been on edge all day in his company. The thought of spending yet another day with him sent her stomach fluttering with nervous tension. 'It's very kind of you, but my mother is visiting from Sydney.'

'Bring her, too,' Adriana encouraged warmly. 'Please, it will be fun to spend another day together, our last on the Gold Coast, for we leave on Monday.'

Stephanie didn't have the heart to refuse. After all, she wouldn't be alone with Raoul. 'I'll check with Celeste and see if she has anything planned, then call you.'

There was a general exodus of people and cars from the theme park, consequently it took a while to gain clear passage onto the highway. Although once there, Raoul was able to pick up speed, and it was after five when he pulled into her driveway.

Extracting Emma, the booster seat, took essential minutes, and Stephanie could hardly refuse Raoul's help. It followed that he came into the house, and Celeste seemed bent on offering him a drink, inquiring about the day, which together with Emma's excited verbal contributions took some time.

He could, she decided with unwarranted cynicism,

have politely declined the drink and retreated within minutes. So why hadn't he?

Worse, he looked very much at ease and far too relaxed for her peace of mind as he conversed with Celeste. Cruising the waterways and an invitation to join them the next day was presented with superb verbal strategy, achieving his objective with a skill she could only admire.

'I'll be delighted.' Celeste beamed warmly. 'Perhaps you'd like to join us for dinner?'

No, Stephanie silently cried, don't do this. But it was too late.

'Raoul may have plans,' she interjected quickly, willing him to refuse.

'No plans,' he returned easily, meeting her gaze as he offered a faint musing smile. 'Thank you. Celeste.'

Fine, let Celeste entertain him. *She* had things to do. Bathing Emma was one of them, not to mention unpacking the holdall of drink bottles, fruit and a number of other comestibles essential to a day out with a young child.

'If you'll excuse me?' She extended her hand to Emma. 'Bathtime, sweetheart.'

Emma's cheerful questions and observations provided a welcome distraction, and afterward Stephanie took time to freshen up. Although she refused to change on the grounds that it would seem as if she'd done so strictly for Raoul's benefit.

'Raoul insisted on buying wine to go with dinner,' Celeste indicated as Stephanie entered the kitchen.

'He should be back soon.' She expertly turned the roast vegetables and slid the pan back into the oven. 'He seems nice, darling.'

Nice? He was many things, but nice? Determined, overwhelming. *Lethal.*

'No comment?' Celeste teased, and caught her daughter's wry glance.

At that moment Raoul returned, and Stephanie busied herself setting the table, then helped Celeste dish the meal.

Her mother was an excellent cook, and Stephanie fought hard to do justice to the food on her plate.

'Do you have family, Raoul?'

Here we go, Stephanie inwardly groaned. The maternal need for background details. She studiously avoided looking at him as she helped Emma with her vegetables.

'Two brothers, Michel and Sebastian. Michel is currently in Australia with his wife. Sebastian and Anneke recently married and are at present touring Europe.'

'Your parents live in France?'

'My mother died a few years ago, but my father resides in the family home and continues to take an active interest in business.'

'Do you live in a big house?' asked Emma, her expression solemn as she waited for his answer.

'Some of the time.'

'Do you have a dog?'

He gave Emma a warm smile. 'Yes, two of them. And two cats, some hens and ducks, geese and a parrot who tells everyone who comes near him to have a happy day.'

Emma's eyes became very round. 'A parrot talks?'

Raoul's eyes gleamed with latent humor. 'Yes,' he enlightened gently. 'He really does.'

'Is it very far away?'

'Raoul lives in Paris, darling. Many thousands of miles on the other side of the world,' Stephanie elaborated.

'Can we come visit?' Emma ventured, innocent of distance.

'I would like that.'

'Shall I serve dessert?' Stephanie queried as she rose to her feet and began stacking cutlery and plates.

A delicious lemon pie was an excellent complement, and she waived Celeste's offer to take care of the dishes.

'You cooked, I'll do the dishes,' she said firmly.

'I agree,' Raoul added as he stood and pushed in his chair. 'You go and sit down. I'll help Stephanie.'

He probably hadn't cleaned a dish in his life. 'Thanks,' she said sweetly. 'You rinse, I'll stack the dishwasher, then you can attack the pots and pans.'

He shot her a dark gleaming glance, almost as if he divined her thoughts, and set about proving her wrong with quick deft thorough movements she found hard to keep pace with. He scoured pots and pans with considerable skill, and when they were all done he wiped down the sink bench, then leaned one hip against the bench and watched her finish up.

'Why don't you go put Emma to bed, while I make coffee?'

It was worth it just to watch those beautiful dark blue eyes dilate and pink color her cheeks. As long as she was angry he didn't have anything to lose, he determined as he caught hold of her chin and possessed her mouth in a brief hungry kiss.

'How dare you?' she whispered furiously, and heard his quietly drawled response,

'Easily.'

She walked from the kitchen without offering a further word, and when she returned he was seated comfortably opposite Celeste, conversing as if he'd known her mother for years.

It was an acquired trait, an entrepreneurial strategy someone kindly disposed would term *charm*. Was it genuine? Celeste seemed to think so, and her mother was no fool when it came to judging character.

'If you'll excuse me, I must leave,' Raoul intimated and rose to his feet. He took hold of her mother's hand and lifted it to his lips. '*Merci*, Celeste, for the meal and your company.'

'I'll see you to the door.' A few minutes and he'd be gone, then she could relax.

He was close, much too close as she preceded him down the hallway, and before she had a chance to open the door he cradled her face and took possession of her mouth in a kiss that tugged at the very depths of her heart.

When he lifted his head she could only look at

him, her breathing as unsteady as her rapidly beating pulse.

'*Bonne nuit, mon ange,*' he bade gently. 'Until tomorrow.' He pressed the pad of his thumb to her lower lip. 'I'll be here at nine.' His mouth curved with sensuous warmth. 'Sleep well.'

He opened the door and moved lightly down the steps to his car, and Stephanie watched as he slid behind the wheel, then reversed down the driveway.

She closed the door, secured the locks, then reentered the lounge.

Celeste wisely didn't comment on the faint color tinging her daughter's cheeks. Instead she mentioned a new social club she'd joined in Sydney, discussed two recent movies and refrained from mentioning Raoul's name. At ten, she stifled a faint yawn, then indicated the need for an early night.

Stephanie followed her down the hallway, closing lights as she went, and in her own room she stripped off her clothes, then indulged in a leisurely shower before slipping into bed to lay staring at the darkened ceiling.

She must have slept, because when she woke sunlight was streaming through chinks in the wooden shutters at her window.

A tap at her door brought her sitting up in bed, and Celeste entered with a cup of coffee in her hand.

'Morning, darling. I thought I should wake you. It's after eight.'

Oh hell. 'Raoul will be here at nine.' She threw

aside the bedcovers and reached for her robe. 'Where's Emma?'

'Watching one of her videos. She's had breakfast, and I've packed the holdall with most of the things I think she'll need.'

Stephanie took a sip of the strong, sweet coffee and felt its reviving effect. 'Thanks, Celeste. I'll grab something to eat, then change.'

Stephanie chose fatigue-style beige shorts, a pale blue singlet top and slid her feet into trainers. Makeup was a thorough application of sunscreen cream, a light dusting of powder, and lipstick.

Raoul arrived at nine, looking ruggedly attractive attired in casual navy shorts and a white short-sleeved polo shirt. He was fit and tanned, with the muscular build of a man who enjoyed exercise and physical fitness.

It was easy to imagine him playing tennis, racquetball, or training in martial arts. He had the look, the physique, and displayed an aura of control.

It was a beautiful day, the sun warm, with just the slightest breeze stirring the palm fronds and tree leaves.

'Going on a boat,' Emma relayed during the drive to Marina Mirage.

A very large luxury boat, Stephanie saw as Bruno led them through the security gate and indicated the berth where the cruiser lay moored.

For the wealthy tourist, private charter was ideal. Captain and crew, plus catering staff ensured a very pleasant excursion without any of the attending hassle.

Celeste took delight in Lucia, and the little girl reciprocated twofold.

'You remind her of her beloved Nonna,' Adriana confided as they settled in the spacious midsection fitted and furnished as a luxurious lounge.

It was evident Raoul and Bruno shared the camaraderie of long friendship, and Stephanie felt her pulse race each time she met his gaze.

He stirred her emotions in a way no man had ever done before. And he knew. It was there in the faint gleam in his eyes, the sensual pull of his mouth as it curved to form a smile.

Throughout the day he made little attempt to touch her, and then it was merely a light brush of his hand on her arm. Emma was generous in her affection, trusting with the unaffected instinct of a child. As far as her daughter was concerned, he was Santa Claus and the Easter Bunny rolled into one.

And you, a persistent little gremlin taunted. What is he to you?

Someone, she conceded cynically, whom she need regard with caution. There was the fear of being hurt, of being let down. And having to pick up the pieces. She'd done it once, and she didn't want to do it again.

Don't think about it, she chastised silently. Enjoy the day for what it is—the company of charming people—and just *be.*

The captain cruised the coastal waterways, the

main Nerang river and the larger inland canals. So many beautiful homes lined the water frontage, many with large cabin cruisers moored at individual jetties. Landscaped gardens, huge stands of palm trees and swimming pools.

The captain gave a commentary on various landmarks, and relayed anecdotes about several different men who had made and lost fortunes during the spasmodic ''boom and bust'' cycles over the years.

After lunch the cruiser headed through the main channel to Sanctuary Cove, then retraced its path via Couran Cove, Stradbroke Island, passed Seaworld theme park, and slid into its berth at Marina Mirage shortly after six.

It had been an incredible day, and Stephanie said so, thanking Bruno and Adriana as they disembarked.

'Please, join us in our apartment for an hour or two.' Adriana issued the invitation with warm enthusiasm. 'I can make a salad, the men will cook steaks on the open grill.'

'But you're leaving tomorrow, you must need to pack—'

'Only a few things,' Adriana assured. 'It is easier to have a wardrobe in each of our apartments. Please, it would give us pleasure for you to visit for a while.'

'The girls are tired,' Stephanie indicated. 'It's been a long day for them.'

'I don't think an hour will make much difference,' Celeste offered as they cleared the security gate and entered the shopping complex.

Two against one, Stephanie reflected wryly. Make

that three, she mentally adjusted as she caught her daughter's expression. Held in the curve of Raoul's arm the little girl looked enchanting, her gold-blond hair so fair against the darker features of the man who carried her.

Seared steaks, fresh salads, eaten with a crusty baguette cut in thick slices, and washed down with a light wine, then followed by coffee made for a appetizing repast, and a fitting relaxed end to the day.

It was almost eight when Raoul drew the car to a halt outside the house, and he released a sleeping Emma from her booster seat, then carried her indoors.

'Third door on the left,' Stephanie instructed, leading the way down the hall. 'I'll change and put her to bed.'

Five minutes later she entered the lounge. 'Can I get you some tea, coffee? A cold drink?'

'Not for me, darling,' Celeste declined, and Raoul shook his head.

'Thanks, but no. I must get back to the hotel. I have some work to do before I catch the early morning flight down to Sydney.'

He was leaving? For how long? And why did she suddenly feel *empty?*

'I'll be back Wednesday evening, Thursday if I encounter any delay.'

He turned to Celeste and bade her good-night, and Stephanie saw him to the door.

'Thanks for a lovely day.'

His smile caused her toes to curl. 'I will phone from Sydney.'

She met his mouth without conscious thought, angling her head to fit his, in a kiss that was dazzling in its intensity, and all too brief.

CHAPTER SEVEN

STEPHANIE deliberately sought a hectic work schedule to ensure there was little time to focus much thought on Raoul. For eight hours each day she was mostly successful. Nights were the worst, for no matter how hard she tried, his image came far too readily to mind.

He even managed to invade her dreams, and more than once she woke in a state of restless anticipation only to discover the image in her mind was precisely that…an image.

He rang twice, relatively brief calls which were confined to inquiries about her day, and Stephanie was able to elicit only that he was deeply involved in delicate negotiations that could delay his return.

Flowers were delivered to her office on Tuesday, with the words ''Missing you, R'' on the card. Stephanie kept them at work where the air conditioning helped keep them fresh.

Deciding what to wear to the gala dinner on Saturday evening caused a thorough appraisal of her wardrobe, and she withdrew three suitable gowns, then discarded each one of them.

What she needed, she determined, was something really spectacular…not flamboyant, but quietly and expensively spectacular.

She found it at an exclusive boutique. A figure-hugging design in black with thin jeweled straps, and the saleslady's approval merely added to her own. The price tag was astronomical, but worth every cent, she assured as she arranged for the hemline to be altered.

So far, the marketing strategy for the film was on schedule, and she made a note to ring Alex Stanford. She really wanted a preview of the shots he'd taken.

Wednesday evening Stephanie arranged for Sarah to baby-sit while she and Celeste went to a movie, a charming tale with an all-star cast featuring English women living in Italy during World War II. Afterward they stopped for coffee in one of several boutique cafés lining a trendy street current in vogue at Broadbeach.

'I'm so pleased to see you enjoying a social life, darling,' Celeste said gently as they waited for their order.

'You mean Raoul,' Stephanie responded without preamble.

'Yes.'

She shook her head in silent negation, assuring, 'It isn't going to happen.'

'I think you should leave your options open.'

A teasing smile curved her lips. 'Celeste, are you suggesting I sleep with him?'

'I'm your mother, darling. Mothers don't encourage their daughters to—'

'Indulge in wild sex,' Stephanie completed, offering Celeste a wicked grin.

'You deserve to be with someone,' Celeste ventured quietly.

A waitress delivered their coffee, and Celeste discussed the movie they'd just seen, the quality of the acting…a subject that lasted for the time it took to savor the superb lattes, before driving the short distance home.

The next day Raoul rang to say he'd be back on the evening flight, and the anticipated pleasure of seeing him again was overwhelming. She'd tried to tell herself she hadn't missed him, but knew she lied.

Friday morning there was another delivery of flowers. Flower, she corrected, unsure how to view the single red rose in its cellophane cylinder. The accompanying card held no message, just the initial *R*.

Lunch was a sandwich eaten at her desk and washed down with bottled water as she ran a check on the photo stills that had arrived by courier from Alex Stanford. He'd noted his selection, and she agreed with him. The shots were good, very good.

The lead actress, Cait Lynden, looked great alongside the two professional models. The lead actor, Gregor Anders, had perfected the right angles to portray himself to the best possible advantage.

Michel Lanier should be well pleased. Especially, with the photo stills of Sandrine. There was something about her, some indefinable quality that commanded a second glance. Add unaffected appeal, exquisite bone structure, and you had a visual winner, Stephanie qualified.

The glossy fashion magazine was due to hit the newsstands next week, the interviews and photo segments would appear in two of the weekly women's magazines the same week. A comprehensive one-on-one interview with Cait Lynden and Gregor Anders was scheduled for the magazine section of the Sunday newspaper in three major states, and television interviews were due to air in two weeks' time.

Then there were the social pages. Cocktail party, the gala charity dinner, to which some of Brisbane and the Gold Coast's social elite were invited, together with photographers and journalists to note and record the event.

It was all part of a well-presented media package aimed to attract public interest, a teaser to encourage paying cinema customers, Stephanie accorded wryly.

It would be nice, she reflected ruminatively, if the movie broke even. Although Michel Lanier could well afford to take the loss.

Filming had finished, and next week the marketing team would attend a private screening and decide which segments should appear as trailers. Meetings, conferences, release dates. It was a comprehensive and exacting project.

Stephanie reached for the phone and made a series of calls, logged data into her computer and ran another check on the table seating for the charity gala dinner to be held in the Grand Ballroom at the Sheraton.

She needed to collect her new gown for the event,

and a call to the boutique ascertained the alterations were complete.

It was almost five-thirty when she parked the car at the Marina Mirage shopping complex. Ten minutes later she emerged from the boutique, an emblazoned carry-bag in hand.

With luck, if the traffic wasn't too heavy, she'd be able to collect Emma from the day care center and be home just after six. Celeste was preparing Emma's favorite meal, and they planned a quiet evening together.

Stephanie stepped onto the escalator and idly scanned the ground floor with its marbled tiles, an attractive water fountain and tables set out for casual alfresco dining.

She glimpsed a familiar male head, and recognized Raoul...in the company of a tall stunningly beautiful woman with dark hair pulled back into a sleek knot, classic features, exquisite makeup and a figure to die for.

Worse, one hand was curled round Raoul's forearm. They looked...*cozy,* Stephanie decided.

Did hearts stop? She was willing to swear hers did. And there was a sudden searing pain in the region of her stomach.

At that precise moment he lifted his head and saw her. For a shocking few seconds his expression assumed a still quality, and he removed the woman's hand from his arm, murmured a few words at her protest and moved toward the base of the escalator.

There was no way Stephanie could avoid him, and

although it took considerable effort she summoned a polite smile as she stepped off.

'Raoul,' she acknowledged with cool formality.

'*Mon ami,* are you not going to introduce us?'

French, Stephanie deduced, huskily feminine and infinitely feline.

'Of course,' Raoul inclined with unruffled ease. 'Ghislaine Chabert. Stephanie Sommers.'

Ghislaine stroked a hand down Raoul's forearm, gifted him a witching smile, then transferred her attention to Stephanie. Her eyes hardened and became cold. 'You are one of Raoul's business acquaintances?'

Oh my. A tigress. With sheathed claws and a mean disposition. 'Michel's,' Stephanie corrected succinctly.

'Stephanie is in marketing.'

Perfectly shaped eyebrows lifted fractionally. 'Ah,' Ghislaine inclined with condescension. 'Sandrine's little movie.'

This could only get worse, and she didn't intend hanging around to discover how much worse. 'If you'll excuse me?' She cast Raoul a measured glance, and inclined her head toward Ghislaine. 'I'm already late to collect my daughter.'

'I'll walk you to your car.'

'Please don't bother.' She stepped to one side and began walking to the set of central escalators that would take her down to the car park.

He said something to Ghislaine in French, brusque

words that were totally incomprehensible, then caught up with Stephanie in a few long strides.

She should have known he'd follow her. Without breaking step she continued toward the escalator, all too aware he was right behind her.

He snagged her arm as she stepped off the escalator and turned her to face him.

'Whatever you're bent on surmising—*don't*,' Raoul warned silkily.

'You haven't a clue what I'm thinking,' Stephanie declared distantly.

'Yes,' he reiterated. 'I do.'

'You read minds?' she flung icily, and glimpsed the cynicism in his smile.

'Yours is remarkably transparent.'

'There is no point to this conversation.'

'*Sacré bleu,*' he swore softly. 'You try the patience of a saint. Ghislaine,' he informed hardily, 'is the daughter of an old family friend, who arrived unannounced, and not by my invitation,' Raoul continued hardily, wanting to kiss her senseless until the doubt, the insecurity, disappeared.

'You don't need to explain,' she declared coolly.

Oh, yes, he did. With concise honesty, right now. 'Ghislaine has booked herself into the same hotel. She's not *with* me,' he said with deliberate emphasis. 'She never has been.'

She directed him a level look. 'Why are you telling me this?'

He wanted to smote his fist against something

hard. 'Because Ghislaine is a femme fatale who finds it amusing to play games.'

Stephanie took in a breath and released it as an exasperated sigh. 'I'd love to stop and chat, but I have to pick up Emma.'

'And you don't believe a word I've said.'

She retained his gaze fearlessly. 'You're free to do whatever you like with whomever you please.' She looked pointedly at his hand on her arm.

'You're making obstacles where there are none.'

'No,' she refuted as he released her. 'I'm making it easy.'

Dignity won out every time, she assured silently as she crossed through two rows to where she'd parked her car. Except dignity didn't do a thing for the way her nerves were shredding into numerous strands. Nor did it help ease the painful ache in her stomach.

She unlocked the door and slid in behind the wheel, then she fired the engine and sent the car up to ground level.

Perhaps it was as well she'd planned a quiet evening at home with Celeste and Emma. She needed time to think.

When Raoul rang at eight, she had Celeste tell him she was putting Emma to bed. She didn't return his call.

Her mother wisely maintained a silent counsel, for which Stephanie was grateful. Maternal advice, no matter how well-meaning, wasn't high on her list tonight.

Together they viewed a video, followed by a program on cable, before reaching a mutual agreement to retire.

There were too many images invading her mind to promote sleep, and Stephanie didn't even try. Instead she plumped an extra pillow against the bed head and picked up a book.

Two hours later she snapped off the bed lamp and stared into the darkness.

Tomorrow was going to be a long day, followed by an even longer night. There were press interviews and photographers scheduled to cover the film cast at Movieworld. She needed to take Celeste and Emma to the airport for the midday flight to Sydney. Then there was the gala dinner.

Would Ghislaine inveigle an invitation? It wouldn't be difficult to acquire one. The Grand Ballroom was large, the staff adept at setting up an extra table or two at the last moment, providing seating wasn't already at maximum. All Ghislaine needed to do was have a discreet word in the right ear and pay for the privilege.

Stephanie stifled a muffled curse and thumped her pillow.

The image of Ghislaine *clinging* to Raoul's arm was vivid in her mind. And how had the Frenchwoman known where Raoul was staying?

She vowed it didn't matter. But it did. It mattered a lot. Despite her efforts to prevent it, he'd managed to scale every protective wall she'd erected, and was close to invading her heart.

Raoul's warning returned to haunt her. Ghislaine liked to play games, huh? Well, let the games begin!

It was a wrench depositing Celeste and Emma at the airport, and Stephanie experienced a mixture of acute loss and emotional deprivation as she hugged Emma close in a final farewell as they passed through security. Watching the jet taxi down the runway, then ascend, was never a good idea. Maybe, when Emma grew older, she'd be able to discard the practice. But now, the little girl was so young, so vulnerable...yet so excited and happy to embark on an adventure.

Emma would have a wonderful time, Stephanie assured herself as she slid into the car and drove toward the car park exit.

It was *she* who needed to adjust to an empty house, the lack of childish chatter and laughter. The umbilical cord connecting mother to child, although cut at birth, was never really severed, she mused as she gained the northbound highway.

Stephanie stopped off at home, heated a slice of Celeste's quiche and ate it, checked her answering machine, then she collected a container of commercially bottled water from the refrigerator and returned to her car.

Dedication to the job was a fine thing, and she could easily have delegated an appearance at the Movieworld shoot. Except she considered it important to be present for any on-the-spot decisions. It was precisely that dedication to detail that had seen her rise through the marketing ranks.

Away from the comfort of air conditioning the heat was intense. As the afternoon wore on, dispositions became frayed, artistic temperament increased and the suggestion they move to another location brought voiced dissent from a few.

'It'll add another dimension,' Alex Stanford assured as he packed his camera and hefted the bag over one shoulder.

'Okay,' Stephanie indicated, trusting his judgment. 'See you there.'

She'd almost reached the car when her cell phone rang.

'Not returning my calls is becoming a habit of yours,' Raoul's voice drawled close to her ear.

Her pulse rate picked up and quickened to a faster beat. 'It's been quite a day.'

'I'll pick you up at seven.'

'Please don't,' she responded quickly, aware of the need to be at the hotel early.

'Stephanie.' His voice acquired a warning edge she chose to ignore.

'Once we're seated, I'm off the hook,' she relayed succinctly. 'Prior to that, I'll be working the job. You'll be superfluous.'

'What time do you have to be there?' His slightly accented voice sent a shiver feathering down her spine.

The sound of a car horn distorted audible clarity, and she put a hand over one ear. 'I have to go,' she indicated.

'Six-fifteen?'

She would have argued, endorsing her decision to meet him at the hotel, except she didn't have the time to conduct a verbal sparring match. 'Fine.'

The afternoon was fraught, and by five even the television camera crew were relieved to dismantle equipment and head for their vehicle.

Consequently it was five-thirty by the time Stephanie reached Mermaid Beach, and home. Forty-five minutes in which to shower, wash and dry her hair, apply makeup and dress didn't present an enviable time frame.

With speed and efficiency she managed it…just. The doorbell pealed as she was in the process of attaching ear studs, and she quickly slid her feet into stiletto-heeled pumps, spritzed perfume to a few pulse points, then she caught up her evening purse and headed for the front door.

The breath caught in her throat at the sight of him. It wasn't the dark evening suit, nor the snowy white pin-tucked shirt, but the man himself and the significant aura of power he exuded. There was a sense of strength, an innate quality that had little to do with his muscular frame or chiseled facial features.

'We really should leave,' Stephanie said coolly.

The gown did wonderful things for her, it was precisely the reason she'd seriously challenged the limit on her credit card. Her job called for what she termed "a working wardrobe," yet the motivation for the purchase of this particular acquisition had been personal rather than professional.

'Beautiful,' Raoul accorded gently, and glimpsed pleasure appeared briefly before she masked it.

'Thank you,' she returned solemnly. He made her nervous, and she hoped it didn't show.

No other man had the power to arouse such a complexity of emotions. Why *this* man? she asked silently as they traveled the northbound highway toward Main Beach.

It was a question that increasingly haunted her with each passing day. *What are you going to do about it?* an elusive imp persisted. *Have an affair?* One week of heaven, followed by a lifetime of attempting to deal with it?

A silent bubble of hysterical laughter died in her throat. Never had she been so prey to such a range of ambivalent feelings, swinging like a pendulum from *go for it and to hell with the consequences* to *don't do this to yourself.*

'You're very quiet,' Raoul observed, shooting her a discerning glance as they neared their destination.

'Just a hectic day,' Stephanie revealed evenly. She was still angry with him, but mostly she was angry with Ghislaine.

'Fragile egos, interrupted schedules that went way over time?'

And that only accounted for the *day*. She offered him a rueful smile. 'How did you guess?'

Six-thirty For Seven on the invitations meant there were guests already mingling in the lounge area outside the hotel ballroom.

The prestigious yearly event in aid of charity ensured attendance by the social glitterati, and the very reason why Stephanie had seized the marketing opportunity to have key members of the cast attend. The publicity potential was too good to miss.

Four leading European fashion houses with boutiques in the upmarket Mirage shopping complex had compiled a fashion parade with models displaying the new season's releases.

However, it was the fragile egos that had her running a personal check of the table seatings. The charity organizers had arranged their own tables, but the few set aside for important guests and dignitaries required personal attention.

Stephanie located the tables up front, ran a check on place names, made one change, then returned to the lounge, caught sight of Alex Stanford and crossed to confer with him about the shots she wanted.

'Where are our exalted stars?' Alex queried. 'Bent on making an entrance?'

'Michel and Sandrine have just arrived,' she indicated. 'There they are talking to Michel's brother.' And Ghislaine.

Now why didn't that surprise her?

At that moment the main doors opened and the guests began entering the ballroom. Women wearing designer gowns and sufficient jewelry to warrant security measures, while the men observed the formal evening wear, black tie dress code.

Michel and Sandrine drew near, closely followed by Raoul and Ghislaine.

'You are joining us?'

Stephanie met Raoul's enigmatic gaze and held it. 'Soon. I need to have a word with the photographer.'

Ghislaine slipped an arm through Raoul's and cast Stephanie a brilliant smile. *Mine,* the gesture stated.

The Frenchwoman looked stunning, her gown a strapless, backless masterpiece that shrieked European couturier. A single strand diamond necklace looked expensive, and was matched with a bracelet and ear studs.

Stephanie greeted Michel and Sandrine, acknowledged Ghislaine, then she excused herself and went in search of Alex Stanford.

Five minutes later she entered the ballroom and began weaving her way toward their designated table. There was still no sign of Cait Lynden or Gregor Anders, she saw at a glance. However, Tony the film's director was seated at an adjacent table with the producer, two of the Warner Brothers Movieworld executives and their wives. And Ghislaine.

Whose influence had Ghislaine used to secure a seat at one of the main tables? Raoul? Possibly Michel? Stephanie assured herself she didn't want to know.

She slid into her seat just as the lights flickered indicating the opening speech was about to begin, and suddenly there was Cait Lynden and Gregor Anders, their progress to the head of the room spotlighted and captured by a clutch of professional photographers.

It was almost amusing, Stephanie alluded wryly,

if only one could manage to see the humour in the situation. Michel was under siege from the expressive attention of the lead actress, who, it appeared, was intent on displaying subtle designs on Sandrine's husband.

Whereas on the adjacent table, Ghislaine was doing her very best to garner Raoul's attention.

The charity chairwoman gave an introductory speech, followed by a word from the mayor, then the waiters emerged bearing trays containing the starters.

The food was attractively presented, but Stephanie merely forked a few morsels, and barely did justice to the main course.

'Some more water?'

Stephanie cast Raoul a polite glance. 'Thank you.'

His eyes darkened fractionally, and he restrained the desire to rattle her composure.

The announcement the fashion parade was about to begin precluded the need for silence, and Stephanie was grateful as the room lighting dimmed and spotlights highlighted the catwalk.

Beautiful clothes in several categories, although emphasis was placed on after-five and evening wear, specifically aimed, Stephanie conceded, for the society women in attendance. Expertly choreographed and commentated, the parade provided forty minutes of glitz and glamour.

There was a time lag before the serving of dessert and coffee. It was then the photographers sought to capture their shots, and she employed diplomacy when Cait Lynden instructed a photo be taken with

Michel, who had given prior instructions that any photo taken of him must also include his wife.

'Both Lanier brothers?' Alex Stanford suggested, motioning for Raoul to join Michel and Sandrine.

'Why not include the marketing manager?' Raoul countered smoothly as he stood to his feet. He held out a hand. 'Stephanie?'

'Alex has been instructed to involve me in a group shot with Tony, the producer and the Warner Brothers Movieworld executives.'

Raoul was too skilled in psychological manipulation to condone defeat. 'I imagine Alex is not limited to the number of film rolls he is able to use?'

Alex, sensing a display of wills and mildly amused by its possibilities, merely endorsed Raoul's suggestion by motioning her into position. 'Let's do it, Stephanie.'

To refuse would seem churlish, and she slid to her feet and stood where Alex positioned her, between Sandrine and Raoul with Michel at his wife's side.

Raoul slipped an arm along the back of her waist, and she stood completely still as all her senses kicked into vibrant life.

She was suddenly conscious of every breath she took, and consciously regulated each and every one of them in a bid to reduce the rapid beating of her heart. She could feel the thud of it reflected in the pulse at the base of her throat, her wrists, and the warmth it generated deep inside.

Even her skin seemed acutely sensitized, and she

was willing to swear heat whispered through every vein in her body.

Stephanie almost jumped as his fingers caressed the base of her spine, then moved to the back of her waist in a slow, soothing pattern. Was he aware of the effect he had on her? She hoped not.

'One more,' Alex called, and the flashbulb caused a second's blindness.

'Not so difficult, *oui?*' Raoul murmured musingly as they moved back to their table.

'Do you always get your own way?'

'Yes.'

Guests were moving between tables, socializing briefly with friends and acquaintances before the evening wound down to a conclusion.

Stephanie placed a hand over her glass as he lifted a bottle of wine. 'No, thanks.'

Raoul's smile held sensual warmth. 'The need for a clear head?'

'I rarely drink,' she said quietly, frozen into immobility as he lifted a hand to her cheek and trailed his fingers down to the edge of her mouth. Her eyes widened, their depths darkening as the pupils dilated, and she barely controlled an involuntary shiver as he traced the sensitive chord of her neck and rested briefly in the hollow there.

'Stephanie, I need you to be part of the executive group shot,' Alex Stanford intruded, and the mesmeric spell was broken.

Thankfully, she assured silently as she followed the photographer. It wasn't easy to slip away, for the

film director and producer were in a gregarious
mood, so too were the Warner Brothers' executives,
and almost fifteen minutes passed before she was
able to leave.

Sandrine was not in evidence, nor were the two
dignitaries who comprised part of the table seating.
Raoul and Michel were engrossed in conversation,
and seated in an empty chair...*her* chair...was
Ghislaine.

It would have been polite for the Frenchwoman to
move, but Ghislaine obviously had no intention of
observing conventional good manners.

Stephanie collected her glass, and crossed to another table where two of her associates were seated.
If Ghislaine wanted to command Raoul's attention,
she could have the figurative floor all to herself.

It didn't help that Samuel Stone occupied a chair
next to the one empty seat at the table. Nor that he'd
generously imbibed of the wine, and had moved on
to spirits. Maybe if she ignored him, he wouldn't
even notice her presence.

Fat chance, Stephanie accorded within seconds.
She'd merely exchanged one awkward situation at
one table for a worse situation of a different kind at
another table.

'Darling Stephanie.' Samuel leaned close, much
too close, and lifted his glass. 'I salute you.'

'Thank you.' She wasn't quite sure what he was
saluting her for, but it seemed prudent to agree with
him.

'You're good,' he continued. 'Very, very good,

darling.' He curved an arm over her shoulders. 'Why don't you come work for me?'

Wouldn't that be a move in the wrong direction, she derided silently.

Instinct caused her to glance toward Raoul. He looked completely at ease, his posture relaxed, his features portraying studied interest. Yet almost as if he could sense her attention his gaze shifted, and his gaze locked with hers.

She saw him say something to Michel and Sandrine, then he rose to his feet and moved toward her.

CHAPTER EIGHT

STEPHANIE indicated her intention to leave. 'If you'll excuse me?'

If Raoul thought she'd calmly return to their designated table and watch Ghislaine continue her *clinging vine* performance, he was sadly mistaken!

She'd only taken two steps when he drew level.

His eyes were dark. Too dark, she discerned.

'We've been invited, together with Michel and Sandrine, to party on at the hotel's nightclub. I understand the cast, studio marketing and advertising executives intend to transfer there.'

She looked at him carefully. 'And Ghislaine?'

Something moved in those dark depths, and a muscle tensed at the edge of his jaw. 'She's free to do as she pleases.'

'As I am,' Stephanie responded quietly. 'Now, if you'll excuse me, I need to freshen up.'

'Damn.' The curse fell from his lips with restrained anger. 'Why would I choose to spend time with her, when I prefer to be with you?'

'She's French, gorgeous, eminently suitable and she adores you,' she responded flippantly.

'And if I do not adore her?'

The mere thought of him adoring another woman made her feel slightly ill. Yet some irrepressible imp goaded her to offer, 'Consider the amalgamation of two family fortunes.'

'Go freshen up, Stephanie,' he drawled. 'Before I say something regrettable.'

Without a further word she turned and made her way toward one of the exit doors.

'Mind if I join you?'

Stephanie caught the faintly wry tone, glimpsed an edge of exasperation evident and offered Sandrine a wicked smile.

'On an escape mission?'

'You've got it in one.'

A queue in the powder room meant they were in for a short wait.

'Now that filming is over, I imagine you'll be returning to New York,' she began in an attempt at conversation.

'We're flying down to Sydney tomorrow for a few days before heading home on Tuesday…sans Cait Lynden,' she concluded quizzically.

A faint chuckle emerged from Stephanie's throat. 'Like that, huh?'

'Oh, yes.'

Even an unsuspecting bystander couldn't have misinterpreted the lead actress's marked play for Michel's attention. Although having witnessed the occasional exchanged look between Michel and his wife, she doubted Sandrine had anything to worry about.

'For what it's worth, Ghislaine has been on the scene for several years,' Sandrine offered gently.

'The Lanier men don't waste time going after what they want. If Raoul wanted Ghislaine, he would have had a ring on her finger by now.'

'It really doesn't interest me.'

'Doesn't it?'

Was Sandrine especially intuitive? Or was she merely attempting to elicit an indication of Stephanie's feelings?

Somehow the latter didn't ring true. She was spared a response as a stall became empty and the actress moved forward to occupy it.

Minutes later they took time for makeup repairs, then together they emerged to find Raoul and Michel examining the picturesque waterfall adjoining the lounge area. Cait, Gregor and Ghislaine stood close by.

'Into battle,' Sandrine murmured, and Stephanie successfully hid a faint smile. *Battle* could very well be the operative word if Cait Lynden continued to monopolize Michel's attention,

The hotel nightclub was situated on the next floor, and the exclusive club was alive with people. Funky music emitted from strategically placed speakers, and subdued lighting added to the overall ambience.

Stephanie hadn't frequented a nightclub since she broke up with Ben, and she was quite content to observe rather than participate.

Cait and Ghislaine made a good pair, she determined as she observed each young woman's attempt to encourage Raoul and Michel onto the dance floor.

'Do you want to escape the performance?'

There were any number of females present who would have drooled at the chance to dance with Gregor Anders. Stephanie wasn't one of them.

'Your bête noire has just entered the milieu,' Gregor intoned cynically. 'Do you really want to have to fend him off?'

A surreptitious glance confirmed Samuel Stone's presence, and if she had to choose between the two, Gregor got her vote.

'This really isn't my scene,' she assured as he drew her onto the crowded floor.

'So...treat you gently?'

Her faint laugh was genuine. 'No fancy flamboyant moves,' she warned.

'We could try for up close and personal.'

'Considering the beat of the music, that might not be wise.'

'Where's your sense of adventure?' He pulled her close, and expertly led her through a set of basic steps. 'Well, well,' he murmured close to her ear. 'An update in the manhunting stakes sees Cait cast aside by Michel, who has very wisely made it clear he prefers his wife. And there,' he revealed with theatrical timing. 'We have Raoul giving Ghislaine the flick.' He executed a sweeping turn. 'Now we see the elder Lanier brother beating a path toward us. *You*, my dear, appear to be his target.'

'You're mistaken.'

'Want me to play the shining knight?'

'And have those good looks marred?' she countered, and saw him wince.

'I agree. He's a formidable quarry, in more ways than one. Prepare yourself for takeover.'

Stephanie sensed Raoul's presence a few seconds before he drew level, and her whole circulatory system immediately went into overdrive.

She was willing to swear the blood traveled faster through her veins, and her pulse seemed to jump to an accelerated beat. Even her skin's surface prickled with awareness.

'Do you mind, Gregor?' The voice was a deep drawl that held an edge of steel.

Gregor didn't mind at all. He didn't even feign reluctance. So much for the shining knight offer!

'Be my guest.' The words scarcely left his lips than he faded away between the milling patrons.

The music changed from fast and funky to a soulful ballad, and Raoul drew her close against him.

She should object, and pull back a little, but although the mind dictated, her body chose not to obey. She fit perfectly, and there was a part of her that wanted to lean in and just drift.

For a few minutes she did just that, succumbing to an insidious sensuality that intensified with every passing second. Treacherous, primal, *raw*.

The music changed, and she told herself she was glad. Sexual passion in any form wasn't on her agenda. Especially with a man who lived on the other side of the world, and to whom she was merely a passing fancy. Someone to be his social partner and occupy his bed for a limited time.

Even the thought of engaging in sex with him

turned her bones to liquid. Instinct warned that this man would not take his pleasure without thought for hers, and just thinking how he could pleasure her was sufficient to set her pulse racing into overdrive.

Dangerous. Infinitely dangerous, she perceived, unwilling to admit even to herself that with each passing day her resistance was gradually ebbing away.

Was he aware of it? Probably, she conceded, for he was far too attuned to her psyche. Having someone anticipate her thoughts, her actions, made her feel uncomfortable. And guarded.

'We're leaving,' Michel indicated, then he turned toward his brother. 'I'll ring you early Monday morning.'

Raoul inclined his head, and Sandrine leaned forward to touch her cheek to Stephanie's, murmuring 'good luck' as she did so, then drawing away she offered Stephanie a warm smile. 'I hope we get to meet again.'

Words, sincerely meant, but expressing a desire for something that would probably not eventuate. Nevertheless, Stephanie returned the words in kind.

'Stephanie!'

Oh Lord, Samuel Stone, more than a little the worse for wear and on a mission, from his determined expression.

'Dance with me.'

'We were about to leave,' Raoul drawled. 'Perhaps another time?'

Not if she could avoid it. 'Sorry, Samuel.'

'C'mon, Stephanie.' He reached out and caught her arm in a viselike grip. 'Let's give it a whirl.'

'I think not, my friend.' Raoul's voice was deceptively quiet, like steel encased in silk.

Samuel's expression assumed alcohol-induced belligerence. 'Staked a claim, have you?'

Raoul didn't move an inch, but the air suddenly seemed charged with threatening promise. 'Yes,' he acceded with hard inflexibility.

For a heart-stopping few seconds Stephanie froze, unaware of the room, the people, the noise. There was only Raoul, and the indomitable power he portrayed.

Then Samuel released her arm and spread his hands in a conciliatory gesture. 'Your round, ice princess,' he conceded with deliberate mockery, and melted through the crowd.

'Trouble, darling?' Ghislaine arched delicately.

Lose one, gain one, Stephanie accorded silently. 'Nothing to be concerned about,' she said with an edge of mockery.

'Raoul is very good at defending a woman's honor.' Ghislaine cast him a sultry look. 'Aren't you, *mon ami?*'

'Good night,' Stephanie issued when Raoul didn't answer.

'Oh really, darling?' The pout had been practiced to perfection. 'You're leaving so soon? It's early.'

'For you, possibly,' Stephanie remarked steadily. 'But my day began at dawn this morning.'

'Why interrupt Raoul's enjoyment? I am sure you can take a taxi home.'

'No,' he said with chilling softness. 'That isn't an option.'

'Aren't you taking chivalry a little too far?' Ghislaine queried with a hint of disdain.

Raoul placed an arm along the back of Stephanie's waist. '*Bon nuit,* Ghislaine.'

His tone held indolence and the smoothness of silk.

'I'm impressed,' Stephanie declared as he propelled her toward the entrance. 'Do you do this often?'

'Do what, precisely?'

They exited the nightclub and made their way to the lift that would take them down to the car park.

'Defend one woman and destroy another, both at the same time.'

'You have a way with words,' he alluded cynically, and she cast him a dazzling smile.

'It's one of my talents,' she assured.

'I have to fly down to Sydney tomorrow,' Raoul informed as they rode the lift. 'I had a call this afternoon to say the deal has been finalized and the contract will be ready for my signature on Monday.'

Her heart plummeted. Finalizing the deal meant there was no reason for him to stay.

'Will you take a direct flight from Sydney to Paris?'

He cast her a sharp glance, saw the carefully composed features, and noted the visible pulse beat at the base of her throat. Not so composed, he conceded with satisfaction.

'I intend returning to the coast Monday evening.'

She wasn't aware she'd been holding her breath, and she released it slowly, evenly. 'I see.'

They reached the car, and Raoul freed the lock. 'Do you?'

Now, there was a question. How did she answer it without incriminating herself? Best not to even try, she bade silently as she slid into the passenger seat.

He fired the engine and eased the car toward the main exit, then gained the divided road that led to the main southbound highway.

'No answer?'

'There isn't one,' she said simply.

Brightly colored neon detailed shops and cafés as they passed through the heart of Surfers Paradise.

Motels lined both sides of the highway. It was a vibrant colorful city, geared for the tourist dollar, and offered a multitude of entertainment services.

The flow of traffic at this hour of the night was smooth, and it seemed only minutes before they drove through Broadbeach and entered the fringes of Mermaid Beach.

Raoul brought the car to a smooth halt in her driveway, and cut the lights and the engine.

She released her seat belt, then undid the door clasp and slid out, aware he was duplicating her actions.

'There's no need for you to come in.'

He crossed around and held his hand out for her keys. 'Yes, there is.'

At that precise moment she was prepared to agree with Ghislaine. There was a limit to chivalry.

'I'll be fine,' she assured as he unlocked the door and switched on the lights.

'Are you afraid of me, *cherie?*'

Confrontation was admirable, but right now she wasn't sure she cared for it. 'No,' she answered honestly.

It was herself she was afraid of. Afraid that if he kissed her, she might not be able to control her emotions. And if she relinquished that control, she knew precisely where it would lead.

To experience his lovemaking would be...incredible, she qualified. To take him to her bed, and wake to his touch... Dare she?

She looked at him, saw the strength evident, the heat carefully banked, and felt her body leap with answering warmth.

Stephanie made her way through to the lounge, aware he followed close behind. Her composure was rapidly falling into shreds, and she mentally chastised herself. Nerves were hell and damnation. Raoul was just a man, like any other.

A lot you know, she silently derided. It's four years since I was intimate with a man, and I feel gauche, awkward...dammit, *scared* in a way that has nothing to do with *fear.*

This could, he cautioned, disintegrate in a second. She was a complex mix that comprised integrity and honesty, with a well of passion a man could drown in if he wasn't careful. Yet there was also deep-seated pain and distrust.

'Go make some coffee,' he said quietly.

So he wasn't about to seduce her…at least, not right now. She should have felt relieved, but instead there was a sense of delaying the inevitable, and that in itself only worsened the state of her nerves.

Stephanie entered the kitchen, filled the carafe with water and set it into the coffeemaker, measured out and added ground coffee beans.

'I imagine Celeste has rung to confirm their safe arrival?'

He'd moved so quietly she hadn't heard a sound, and she spared him a quick glance as she extracted two cups and saucers from a cupboard.

'Yes. Everything's fine.' A few steps to the refrigerator to retrieve milk. 'Would you like something to eat?'

When she closed the refrigerator door he was there, and she felt her eyes widen as he took the milk container from her hand and set it on the bench.

'You. Just you.'

He didn't give her time to protest as he drew her close, and his mouth fastened on hers in a slow evocative tasting that became a feast of the senses.

Impossibly sensual, it dispensed all rational thought as she angled her head and indulged in an emotional ride that swept her high to a place where there was only the man, the moment…and desire.

Dear heaven, it was all she could do not to slip

her hands beneath his jacket and tear the garment free. Loosen the buttons on his shirt in her need to touch his skin. To feel the warmth, the pulsing life of muscle and sinew, to savor the taste of him. And have him taste her.

The kiss deepened into possession as his hand slid to her derriere and pulled her close against him. His arousal was a potent force, electrifying and primal as she instinctively reached for him.

She felt a tremor race through his body, and for an instant she gloried in the power, the supreme, albeit brief moment of having him at her mercy.

Then the control was all his as he took his mouth from her own and began trailing a tantalizing path down the edge of her neck, drifting to tease the hollows at the base of her throat, before slipping low to the soft swell of her breast.

A beaded shoestring strap slid off one shoulder, and a faint groan escaped from her lips as he bared one breast, then shaped it, stroking the creamy contour until she thought she'd go mad.

His lips sought the sensitive peak and tantalized it with his tongue, grazing it with his teeth as he held her on the knife edge between pleasure and pain.

When he took the distended peak into his mouth and suckled she arched up against him as sensation arrowed through her body.

It was almost more than she could bear, and she made no protest as Raoul slid an arm beneath her knees and lifted her high into his arms.

His mouth returned to claim hers, and she wound

her arms around his neck as she kissed him back, exulting in the sensation he was able to evoke.

It was relatively easy to discover which bedroom was hers. Feminine in soft peach and pale mint green, an antique bed, and numerous lacy pillows stacked against the headboard.

He shrugged off his jacket, discarded the bow tie and paused to brush light fingers down her cheek as she sought to free the buttons on his shirt.

In tandem they slid off shoes, then Raoul sought the zip fastening at the back of her gown and slid it free.

She was beautiful, slender curves, delicate bone structure and pale skin. Lacy bikini briefs were the only item of clothing protecting her from total nudity, and he shrugged off his shirt and dispensed with his trousers in two fluid movements.

Stephanie could only admire his physique. The well-honed muscular chest and shoulders, the taut waist and flat stomach.

The state of his arousal gave her a bad moment, and her insides involuntarily clenched at the thought of accommodating him.

He curled a hand round her nape and shaped her head as he took possession of her mouth, kissing her with such eroticism she almost cried at the sweet sorcery of his touch.

One tug was all it took to pull the covers from the bed, then he tumbled her down onto the sheeted mattress and knelt over her.

His eyes were dark and slumberous, and his

strength was a palpable entity as he buried his mouth against her neck.

Stephanie lifted her arms and linked them at his nape, only to have him gently disengage them and carefully place them above her head.

She felt a tremor race through her body as he traced a path to her breast, explored at leisure, then trailed down to the soft indentation at her waist.

A faint gasp escaped her lips as he moved lower, and she whimpered out loud at the path traced by the tip of his tongue.

Raoul took intimacy to a new level, evoking a response from her that was wild and wanton. Libidinous, she added, as sensation spiraled through her body, taking her higher than she'd ever been before.

Dear heaven. If this is what he could do with his mouth, how on earth would she survive when he took possession? Go up in flames? Self-destruct?

Both, Stephanie acknowledged a long time later as she lay cradled against him on the edge of sleep.

Every nerve ending had flared into impassioned life as he'd begun a slow invasion, stirring her emotions to fever pitch with long hungry kisses that dispensed with any inhibitions. She'd met and matched his rhythm in a wild pagan dance that surpassed her wildest imagination.

She'd thought he might vacate her bed, shower, then dress and leave.

Instead he curved her close in against him and

stroked her hair, pausing every now and then to brush light fingers across her cheek.

Her body ached, and she was willing to swear she could still *feel* him deep inside.

She wasn't conscious of drifting off to sleep, except she must have, for she came slowly awake at the soft tracing movement at her waist. Fingers slid over one hip and brushed against her thigh, and she shifted restlessly as he began an evocative pattern.

Stephanie leaned forward and nipped the skin close to one male nipple, and had the satisfaction of hearing his intake of breath.

'So you want to play, hmm?'

In one fluid movement he pulled her on top of him, and she arched back in a supple feline movement.

'You woke me,' she protested teasingly, loving the feel of his hands as they shaped her body, her breasts, and took a tantalizing path down to where she straddled him.

'Now I have your full attention?'

Oh, yes, he had that. She wriggled a little, and took pleasure in his husky groan, the heat of his arousal pressing against her.

With provocative intent, she moved a little, causing a sexual friction that was just as electrifying for him as it was for her.

In one swift movement he curved a hand around her nape and pulled her head down to his, taking possession of her mouth in a manner that left her weak-willed and malleable.

When he released her she rose with graceful fluidity, then carefully positioned herself and took him deep inside.

She had control, and she used it mercilessly as she rode him hard and fast, then eased to a slow erotic pace that had him growling low in his throat as he rolled her onto her back.

At some stage they both slept, and woke late to the sun streaming in through the curtains.

Together they rose from the bed and showered to-gether...a long shower as Raoul pulled her high against him and she curved her legs over his hips in one final passionate coupling, then they dressed and breakfasted on strong coffee, eggs and toast.

It was after ten when Raoul caught her close and bestowed a lingering kiss. 'I have to leave,' he said gently. 'I'll call you from Sydney.' His smile held a warmth that made her stomach curl. 'Take care, *cherie.*'

Without a further word he slid in behind the wheel of the car, fired the engine, then reversed out onto the road.

Stephanie stood watching until the car was no longer in sight.

CHAPTER NINE

THE day stretched ahead, presenting a number of possibilities. However, the first priority was to put a call through to Celeste.

Stephanie crossed to the phone and punched in the required digits, then listened to Emma relay an excited account of the flight, the drive with her beloved 'Poppa,' playing with Jake the dog and a visit to the beach as soon as she woke from her afternoon nap.

'Sounds like fun,' Stephanie said lightly when Celeste came back on the line.

'It is,' her mother assured. 'And you, Stephanie? Did everything turn out well last night?'

Now there was a question she couldn't answer with total honesty! Revealing to your mother that you'd just experienced the best sex in your life, not once but several times in the past eight hours wasn't exactly a confidence she felt inclined to share.

'Really well,' she responded easily. 'We achieved the necessary publicity, there were no mishaps. It was very successful.'

'And Raoul?'

Oh my. 'He seemed to enjoy himself.' A masterpiece in understatement! 'He left this morning for Sydney. Business,' she elaborated.

'But he'll be back?'

'Yes.'

'Good.'

Don't, Stephanie urged silently. It can't go any-where, because there's nowhere for it to go.

'I'll ring tomorrow evening,' she indicated, then added gently, 'Thanks, Mom. I know Emma will have a wonderful time.'

Housework beckoned, the washing and some iron-ing, and when it was all done she went down to the local supermarket and bought milk, bread and a few essentials.

Afterward she curled up in a comfortable chair and indulged in the luxury of reading several chapters of a seven-hundred-page historical saga. The rich tex-ture of the writing kept her enthralled until the nat-ural light began to fade, and she was about to switch on the lamp when the shrill insistent peal of the tele-phone had her reaching for the receiver.

The male voice was deep, husky and the slight accent identified it as belonging undeniably to Raoul. Just the sound of it sent primitive awareness radiating through her body.

'How are you?'

'Fine.'

His throaty chuckle did crazy things to her equi-librium. 'That's it? Fine?'

'What would you have me say?' she countered unsteadily, and wondered if he was aware just how he affected her.

'It can wait, *cherie*.'

There was a part of her that ached to see him again, yet there was also caution and a certain degree of despair. If only she had a casual attitude to sex without needing any meaningful emotional attachment, she could view the interlude for what it was...a brief affair with no strings.

'Michel and Sandrine are joining me for dinner tonight.'

Stephanie curled her fingers over the receiver. 'Enjoy,' she bade lightly. 'What time is your meeting tomorrow?'

'Early afternoon. I'll call you.'

'Okay.'

'Bonne nuit, cherie,' Raoul drawled. 'Sleep well.'

She didn't, of course. There were too many thoughts chasing through her brain for an easy rest, and she woke next morning with the distinct need for a few hours more sleep.

However, the day awaited, and her work schedule was bound to be hectic.

A shower, followed by cereal and fruit, then she changed into a pencil-slim black skirt, added a peach-colored camisole and pinstriped black jacket, tended to her makeup and caught up her keys before heading for the car.

Only to discover she had a flat tire. The curse she stifled was pithy, and adequately described her frustration. Changing tires was becoming a habit, she muttered beneath her breath as she shrugged off her jacket and tossed it onto the passenger seat.

She crossed to the rear of the car, popped the boot, removed the spare tire, the jack and set to work.

After it was done, she retrieved her keys and went back into the house to wash up.

An essential call into the local tire mart to drop off the damaged tire for repair took up valuable time, added to which traffic was heavy, taking at least three changes of lights to get through each intersection, and consequently she was late entering the office.

Coffee, hot, strong and sweet helped, and she went through her diary, made a number of notations, then logged on to her computer.

The interoffice phone rang and she reached for it.

'I have a Miss Chabert on the line,' Isabel revealed. 'She insists on speaking to you personally.'

Ghislaine? What on earth could she possibly want? 'Put her through.'

'Ghislaine,' Stephanie greeted with polite civility.

'Stephanie. We should do lunch.'

Oh, no, we shouldn't! 'I'm really busy right now,' she responded calmly.

'Meet me at the Terraces. One o'clock.'

The imperious demand grated, and she drew in a deep breath, then released it slowly. 'I can't—'

'Be there.'

This was a joke, a very bad joke. It was almost laughable, except instinct warned there was no humor in the situation at all. 'I can't think of a thing we have in common.'

'Raoul.'

'There's nothing to discuss,' she said quietly, and replaced the receiver. Jealousy, she perceived, was an ugly state of mind.

Lunch was a salad sandwich she sent out for, and ate at her desk. Washed down by bottled water, it sufficed as sustenance as she made necessary calls, checked paperwork and determined the film's scheduled release date. It was important to prompt public interest by running the trailers on television and follow-up media coverage in the trade magazines. She made a note to check with advertising.

At three she broke for coffee, qualifying she needed the caffeine to get her through the afternoon. The way things were going, she'd need to take work home.

It was after four when reception alerted a Ghislaine Chabert was at the desk. Stephanie muffled an unladylike curse. She didn't have time for this. Whatever bee Ghislaine had in her bonnet, this was neither the place nor the time to deal with it.

'You told her I'm busy?'

'Miss Chabert insists on seeing you.'

She quickly checked her diary, then made a split-second decision. 'All right. Show her in.' She stood and smoothed a hand over her hair. 'Ring me when my four-thirty appointment arrives.'

Lipstick was an essential repair, and she'd just re-capped the tube when her secretary gave her door a peremptory tap prior to swinging it wide.

The Frenchwoman swept in on a cloud of perfume, expensive couture clothing, her face an exquisitely made-up mask.

Calm, composed, in control, Stephanie reminded herself of the affirmation as she indicated a chair.

'Ghislaine. Do sit down.' She crossed behind her desk and remained standing. With a cool, calculated action she cast her watch a deliberate glance. 'I can spare you five minutes.'

'I'd prefer to stand.'

They faced each other across the desk like two opposing enemies. Stephanie watchful and distinctly wary, while Ghislaine played the haute dame to the hilt.

'Leave Raoul alone. He is *mine*.'

Straight to the point, with as much subtlety as a sledgehammer. Stephanie deliberately arched one eyebrow. 'Really? The purpose of your visit is to warn me off?'

Ghislaine raked Stephanie's slender form with scorn. 'Why else do you think I am here?'

'Are you done?' she posed quietly, already regretting her decision to have Ghislaine enter her office.

'No, I am not nearly done,' the Frenchwoman responded bluntly. 'Raoul didn't come back to the hotel last night. Was he with you?'

'I don't think that qualifies an answer,' she said carefully, and saw Ghislaine's expression harden.

'You are just a diversion, someone new, different,' the other woman said scathingly. *'Temporary.'*

Stephanie felt the anger flare, and sought measured control. A catfight here, now, didn't form part of her agenda! 'I think you'd better leave.'

'Stay away from him.'

'What if he chooses not to stay away from me?'

'Our respective families want us to marry. I intend to see that it happens.'

She caught the vindictiveness, the irrational sense of purpose in those hard dark eyes, and experienced a chill of apprehension. 'Then I must wish you *good luck,*' she said evenly. 'And ask you to leave.'

Almost on cue the phone buzzed, and she picked up the receiver, listened, then replaced it onto the handset.

'My client is waiting.' She crossed to the door, and opened it. 'Goodbye, Ghislaine.'

'Don't underestimate me' was issued as a silky warning as the Frenchwoman exited the office.

Stephanie took a deep breath, very much in need of a minute or two to dispel her anger, then regain a measure of composure.

Ghislaine was a witch, possibly a dangerous witch with a problem. Sandrine's words came to mind, but it offered little reassurance.

Meantime, she had a job to do, and keeping a valued client waiting overlong in reception didn't form part of her plan.

It was after six when she arrived home, the owner of two new tires, for when she'd called in to collect the repaired spare, the young man shook his head.

'Couldn't fix it, ma'am. It'd been cut.' At her faintly puzzled expression, he elaborated, 'Slashed. With a knife, I'd say.'

How? More importantly, *who?* 'I guess I need a new tire.'

'Two, in the front, make 'em even.'

She didn't even blink. 'Can you do it now?'

'We're due to close soon.'

'Please. I really need my car.'

'Okay, for you I'll make an exception. Take a seat.'

Ten minutes later she wrote a check, then slid into the car and drove home.

Indoors, she changed into shorts and a singlet top, then crossed into the kitchen. She'd prepare a tossed salad and have it with some cold chicken, then follow it with fresh fruit.

After she'd shower, pull on a robe, and put in a few hours at the laptop. But first she'd call Celeste and catch up on Emma's day... A ferry ride and a visit to Taronga Park Zoo, she learned, and tomorrow they were going to ride on the monorail.

'You're spoiling her,' Stephanie protested, and heard her mother's chuckle.

'No, we're having fun.'

It was reassuring not to be missed, but she experienced a very real feeling of loss at not hearing her daughter's voice, the hugs, the kisses.

Work, she determined, as she set the laptop onto the dining-room table more than an hour later, would occupy her mind.

It did, and she became immersed in entering data, saving it on disk ready to print out at the office in the morning.

The doorbell ringing startled her, and she checked her watch, wondering who on earth would call in at

nine in the evening without using the telephone to
check it was okay.

The security door was locked, she had a safety
chain on the door, as well as a peephole. There was
no sense pretending she wasn't home, for the lights
indicated otherwise.

The doorbell rang again, jerking her into motion,
and she moved quickly to the front of the house.

One look was sufficient to determine it was Raoul
who stood on her doorstep, and with nerveless fingers she dealt with the chain, the lock and undid the
security door.

'Hi.' As a greeting it was inane, and Stephanie felt
the warmth creep into her cheeks as he let his gaze
roam over the short silk robe, her bare legs, before
returning to settle on her expressive features.

'Were you in bed?'

He sounded indolently amused, and she ran a
check on the tie of her robe, then pulled the edges
more tightly together.

'No,' she said quickly. 'I was working.'

He was something else, his height and breadth of
shoulder impressive. His exclusive brand of cologne
teased her senses, and her eyes were mesmerized by
the sensual curve of his mouth. He'd removed his
jacket and held it hooked over one shoulder.

'Aren't you going to ask me in?' he queried
gently, and she stood aside at once.

'Of course.'

Raoul stepped down the hallway and she followed
him. 'Would you like some coffee?'

He came to a halt in the lounge and turned to face her. 'Not unless you're making some for yourself. Otherwise a cold drink will do fine.'

She went to the refrigerator and fetched a can of cola, pulled the tab, then extracted a glass and handed both to him.

'Did you eat on the plane?' Of course he'd eaten on the plane, she derided silently. It was after nine, for heaven's sake!

He poured the dark sparkling liquid, then took a long swallow. 'Yes.'

'How was your meeting?' She was aware of the need to make polite conversation, and equally aware he found it amusing.

'Successful.' He placed the empty can down onto the bench, and subjected her to a slow, warm appraisal.

'The contract is signed, the deal completed.'

'Then there's nothing to keep you here.'

The glass followed the empty can, and he leaned one hip against the edge of the bench. 'Yes,' he denied indolently. 'There is.'

Something twisted inside her stomach.

His gaze didn't waver, and she felt as if she was teetering close to a precipice.

'*You,*' Raoul stated solemnly.

That was certainly direct. But in what context? Given Ghislaine's venomous revelation, there was only one possibility.

'As a temporary diversion?' she posed, and saw his gaze narrow fractionally.

'A diversion from what?'

'Ghislaine, and your forthcoming marriage.'

He didn't move, but it seemed his long muscular frame uncoiled and became a formidable force.

Stephanie caught a glimpse of the persona he undoubtedly presented in the business arena. There was a dangerous stillness apparent, a waiting, watchful quality that revealed nothing and gave no hint of his reaction.

'Ghislaine possesses a fanciful imagination,' he drawled. 'Fostered by overindulgent parents in a desire to link Chabert to Lanier.' Facial muscles shifted and reassembled over chiseled bone structure. 'A business merger is out of the question, and there are no marriage plans.'

'Ghislaine appears to think differently.'

'And you believed her?' His voice was quiet, deadly.

Her eyes sparked blue fire, and the anger she'd managed to hold at bay for the past few hours rose to the surface. 'She was very convincing.'

'Yes,' he acknowledged cynically. 'I imagine she was.'

'There's no purpose to this,' Stephanie refuted, sorely tried.

'I disagree.'

Her chin tilted. '*Why?* The result remains the same.'

'You're so sure about that?'

I'm not sure about anything, damn you! But even with the most generous heart, I can't see it happening any other way. A proposal and happy-ever-after belong in fairy stories.

'Raoul,' Stephanie commanded unsteadily. 'Go home. Please.' She wanted him out of here, now, before she did something totally stupid. As it was, her eyes ached with repressed emotion. 'I really do have a few hours work ahead of me.'

He looked at her, saw the tiredness, the emotional strain evident, and subdued the anger he wanted to direct against Ghislaine for having caused Stephanie grief.

Without a word he caught hold of her shoulders and pulled her into his arms, curving a hand beneath her nape as he slid the other down to splay over the slight curve of her bottom.

She twisted against him in an attempt to break free, then fought against dissolving into him as his lips sought the vulnerable hollow at the edge of her neck.

'Don't.' The word emerged as a despairing groan. She didn't want this. She couldn't afford the sweet slide into emotional ecstasy, and she doubted her ability to survive the exquisite passion without fragmenting into a hundred shimmering pieces.

How long they stood together she had no idea. There was the sensation of it being right, as if some ephemeral force was at work. And dear heaven, it was so *good* to lean against him, accept his strength, his assurance.

Like this, she didn't care how long it lasted. It was enough he was here, and they had the night. So what if there were too few nights left? The truth was she didn't want to deny herself the ultimate pleasure of shared intimacy with him. Was that so bad?

Slowly, gently, he disentangled her arms and stood back a pace. Then he caught her chin between thumb and forefinger, lifted it, and tried not to drown in those dark sapphire depths.

'Go do whatever it is you have to do to finish on the computer,' Raoul bade easily. 'I'll get the coffee.'

Stephanie opened her mouth to protest, only to close it again. Her lashes swept wide as he tucked a stray lock of hair behind her ear, then he trailed his fingers down the curve of her cheek and let them rest against the edge of her mouth. He leaned down and dropped a soft kiss on the tip of her nose, then he pushed her gently in the direction of the table, and the computer.

It took her almost two hours, and there was a sense of satisfaction in pressing the Save key and transferring the data onto disk.

She'd been conscious of Raoul sprawled comfortably at ease on the large sofa in the adjoining open plan lounge. He had the television on low, and he looked totally relaxed. Every now and then she'd been conscious of him sparing her a watchful glance, and experienced the answering tremor as her body leaped in response.

With automatic movements she closed down the program, then disconnected the power inlet.

She didn't hear Raoul move, and a slight gasp escaped her lips as she felt his hands close over her shoulders.

His fingers began a deep soothing massage of her shoulders and neck muscles, gradually easing out the kinks until she sighed and let her head roll forward in a gesture of total acceptance.

It felt so good, so very good, it was all she could do not to express her pleasure in a purr of gratitude. When he began on her scalp she closed her eyes and surrendered to the magic.

There was little sense of the passage of time, and she made a token protest as his hands slid to her shoulders, then caught hold of her waist.

In one fluid movement he lifted her into his arms and carried her down the hall to the bedroom.

'Raoul—'

'Don't think,' he said huskily as he swept aside the covers and tumbled down onto the bed with her. His lips caressed the edge of her mouth. 'Just feel.'

He discarded his clothes with ease, shrugging out of his shirt, discarding trousers, shoes and socks, briefs, then he gathered her close and began a long, slow loving that had her begging for release.

It was flagrant, evocative, as his mouth took a tor-tuously slow path over every inch of her body. Caressing, tasting, in a supplication that drove her wild. The blood sang in her veins as sensation spi-raled to impossible heights, and he caught her as she fell, only to wreak havoc as he sent her soaring again and again.

Skillful fingers knew where to touch, to stroke, as

he paid sensual homage to every pleasure spot, each heightened nerve ending. Just as she thought she'd experienced it all, he followed the same path in a tasting feast that made her cry out in all-consuming ecstasy.

Her whole body was one pulsating ache, and her response was unrestrained as she captured his head and dragged his mouth to her own.

He took her then, melding his body to hers in one powerful thrust, stayed there, then began a tantalizing withdrawal, before plunging deeper in a slow primal rhythm that built in pace until there was only the raw passion of two lovers in perfect accord.

Afterward they slept, held close in each other's arms in a tangle of sheets as the moon disappeared and the night became shrouded in darkness.

At some stage Stephanie stirred, felt the soothing slide of fingers down her back, and settled comfortably against warm skin and muscle, subsiding easily into relaxed somnolence.

The shrill sound of the alarm was an impossible intrusion, and Stephanie automatically reached out to close it, only to come in contact with a hard, muscular forearm intent on the same task.

'Six-thirty,' a slightly accented male voice drawled with a degree of amusement. 'Time to rise and shine.'

'Shower's mine,' she voiced drowsily, then yelped in shocked surprise as his hand slid down to create renewed havoc, bringing her to orgasm with such tactile skill it stole her breath. 'I think I should get up.'

Raoul's mouth nuzzled the soft hollow at the base of her neck. 'Only think?'

'Affirmative action is essential,' she said weakly, and slid out from beneath his grasp. 'Otherwise I'll be late.'

He rolled onto his back and linked his arms behind his head. Then he smiled, and Stephanie felt the powerful tug of desire.

She couldn't imagine anything she'd rather do than sink down onto the bed and give in to the hunger, the sheer sensual pleasure of his touch. To gift him a similar pleasure.

What would it be like to wake every morning like this after a night of exquisite lovemaking, only to do it all over again?

Sex. She closed her eyes, then opened them again. Very good sex. It wasn't—*couldn't*—be anything more. Could it?

Oh God. What she felt wasn't love. *Was it?* Realization washed through her body, quickly followed by apprehension. *No,* she screamed a silent denial. This wasn't happening.

Raoul observed the play of emotions chase across her expressive features, saw the shocked surprise evident in her eyes before her lashes swept down in a protective veil, and caught the faint tremor as she lifted a shaky hand to tuck back her hair.

His gaze narrowed fractionally as she caught up her robe and made for the en suite.

Minutes later she stepped into the shower stall, turned on the water and picked up the bottle of shampoo. Only to have it taken out of her hand within seconds of wetting her hair.

'You can't—'

'Yes, I can,' Raoul drawled as he poured thick liquid into one cupped palm, then he massaged it over her scalp.

When he was done, he picked up the soap and began smoothing it over her body. It became a teasing, evocative action that brought a groan to her lips.

At this rate, she'd need to forego breakfast. But oh dear Lord, it would be worth it just to savor his touch, to gift him a similar supplication.

'Raoul.' His name silvered from her lips, and anything else she might have said remained locked in her throat as his mouth closed over hers in a kiss that became a possession all of its own.

Nothing else mattered as he slid her arms up to link at his neck, and when he lifted her close she simply held on, exulting in the shape and feel of him, his strength, his earthy taste and raw sexuality.

She could almost believe he was bent on assaulting her senses…in an attempt to achieve what? she wondered idly as she snagged a towel and removed some of the excess moisture from her hair.

Soft color stained her cheeks at the thought of her craven response, and how easily he was able to achieve it. In his arms she became a wanton, eager to sample every sexual delight he cared to introduce.

Toweled dry, she went through the personal rou-

tine, collected fresh underwear, then hurriedly selected an elegant trouser suit, applied makeup,
brushed her hair and slid her feet into high-heeled
pumps.

Stephanie didn't even bother running a check on
the time. It hardly mattered what the clock said,
when it was obvious she was going to be late.

She caught up her bag, crossed to the laptop and
retrieved the disk, then moved toward the front door.

He was right behind her, his holdall in one hand,
his personal laptop in the other. He'd shaved, and in
place of the suit he wore tailored trousers and a dark
polo shirt.

Stephanie crossed to the garage, used the remote
to open the automatic doors, then swore beneath her
breath when she saw her car had a flat tire.
Something she wouldn't have noticed had she not
crossed around to the front passenger side to shift a
garden rake, which seemed to have slid forward and
lay resting against the bodywork of her car.

'Problems?'

Stephanie gestured toward the front wheel. 'This
is the second time I've had a flat tire in two days,'
she vented angrily. 'If this one is slashed, too, I'm
going to report it to the police.'

'Slashed?' Raoul queried with deceptive quiet, and
she inclined her head.

'That's what the guy at the tire mart said. He fitted
two new tires for me last night.' She pushed a hand
through her hair, and stifled an inward sigh. 'I'll get
the spare.'

'Leave it,' he instructed. 'I'll drive you.'

'Dammit, I *need* my car.'

'And collect you from work. Give me the remote module, a spare key to the car and I'll take care of it.'

She opened her mouth to argue, then simply closed it again as he brushed the knuckles of one hand lightly along her jaw.

'No contest, *ma cher.*'

It was easier to do as he said, and as he negotiated traffic she retrieved her cell phone and called reception, alerting her imminent arrival.

Stephanie reached for the door clasp the moment Raoul swept to a halt outside the entrance to her office building, and she uttered a hurried 'thanks' as she slid from the car.

CHAPTER TEN

As MORNINGS went, Stephanie's was a doozy, and losing an hour merely made a bad situation worse. Everything that could go wrong, did. Worse, her secretary had called in sick, and her temporary replacement didn't have a clue.

Coffee, hot sweet and strong helped some, and she prioritized paperwork, telephone calls, and didn't stop until one, when she deemed it sensible to take a lunch break. Otherwise she'd never make it through the afternoon.

There was a café close by, one of a few which catered for staff working in the many tall office blocks in this part of Southport, and Stephanie covered the short distance, choosing a table outdoors.

Numerous spreading tree branches provided shade, and there were bright striped awnings and umbrellas to protect patrons from the heat of the summer's sun.

The food was superb, the service swift, and within a very short space of time she was presented with a chicken and salad focaccia sandwich and a cappuccino.

It was a beautiful day, and from where she sat she could see the park, the sparkling waters of the main channel, and beyond it the architectural white sails of the Marina Mirage shopping complex soared against the background of blue sky. Next to it stood the condominium complex of the beautifully designed Palazzo Versace.

A view, she conceded with warmth, to die for. The café was well patronized, but not sufficiently so to warrant anyone requesting to share her table, and she took time to enjoy the food, the ambience. Entitled, she assured, by virtue of working late at home last night.

Thinking about what had happened *after* she'd closed down the computer last night set every nerve-end tingling alive. Dangerous, she mused, definitely dangerous to focus overlong on the passion Raoul had aroused...and her answering hunger.

Tonight's cocktail party for the marketing executives was a "must attend" function. Although she need only stay an hour, two at the most, and she'd be able to leave.

Stephanie finished her sandwich, drained the last of her cappuccino, then paid her bill at the counter and walked out into the sunshine.

She hadn't covered more than a few steps when a feminine slightly accented voice said her name.

No, please tell me it isn't Ghislaine, she prayed silently, only to turn and discover her prayers unanswered. What on earth was the Frenchwoman doing in this part of town?

'I took the wrong exit from the shopping center,' Ghislaine offered in explanation. 'I was looking for a taxi rank.'

'Way wrong,' Stephanie agreed. 'You can either

retrace your steps to the center and get directions for the right exit, or,' she suggested, wondering why she should be so helpful, 'I can ring the taxi company and have them send a car here.'

'Oh, *here* would be wonderful.'

It took only minutes to organize, and she replaced the cell phone into her bag. 'You'll have to excuse me. I need to get back to the office.'

'Before you go,' Ghislaine began with pseudo sweetness. 'I want to thank you.'

'For what?'

'Discrediting me with Raoul.'

Stephanie's stomach executed a painful somersault at the thought Ghislaine had probably deliberately set up watch on the off chance she'd frequent her usual lunch venue today.

'You managed to do that all by yourself,' Stephanie responded carefully.

'Raoul rang me this morning, suggesting we meet for coffee at the Terraces.' Her eyes glittered with ill-concealed anger. 'I looked forward to a tête-è-tête. Surely my visit to your office was private?'

Stephanie could almost visualize Ghislaine sharpening her metaphorical claws.

'Or do you always run to your men and tell tales?'

Grr. She was inclined to unsheathe her own! However a scene on a public street simply wasn't on her agenda. Silence, in some instances, was more effective than mere words.

'Who are you? A nonentity with no noble breed-

ing, no social standing, *nothing!*' Ghislaine stated
with scathing insolence.

'Whereas you are eminently qualified in each cri-
terion?'

'*Yes,* damn you!'

Stephanie felt her blood heat. 'Sadly, blue blood
and lineage don't necessarily guarantee desire.'

'*Bitch.*' She took a step forward and swung the
palm of her hand, narrowly missing her target as
Stephanie twisted her head to one side.

'Perhaps I should remind you that verbal defa-
mation can warrant legal prosecution, and physical
abuse will land you in court.'

'Raoul belongs to *me.*'

There was no way she was going to stand here and
take any more of Ghislaine's verbal vitriol. Without
a word she stepped forward and began walking.

'Don't you *dare* turn your back on me. I haven't
finished with you!'

She didn't pause, or even bother to look back. A
mistake, she learned seconds later, as something
heavy careened into her back and almost sent her
sprawling to the pavement.

A shoulder bag, she saw as she straightened, and
swung with Ghislaine's weight behind it. 'That
amounted to deliberate assault.'

Ghislaine's attractive features were brittle with
fury. 'Where are your witnesses?' She gave an expressive shrug. 'As far as I'm concerned, you tripped.
Pity you didn't fall.'

This had gone quite far enough! 'You want to go

the distance, Ghislaine? Raoul won't be impressed to learn you paid someone to slash my tires. Not once, but twice.' Her eyebrows rose. 'You didn't think I'd find out?'

'I don't know what you're talking about.'

Stephanie drew breath, and aimed for the kill. 'No? What did you think your scare tactics would do, Ghislaine? Send me running in the opposite direction?' She shook her head. 'I don't frighten that easily.'

'He just wants you for sex!'

'If that's true,' she opined carefully. 'Why me, when you're so willing to service him?'

Ghislaine looked as if she was going to throw the mother of all hissy fits, for her face paled, then tinged pink. Her eyes assumed a glassy look, her mouth thinned, and if it was possible for steam to emit from a human's ears...

'If you weren't on the scene—'

'It would be some other woman,' Stephanie offered. 'Accept it for the truth, and move on.'

'As you will?'

A horn blast close by alerted the taxi's arrival, and Ghislaine stepped across the grass verge and slid into the rear seat. Seconds later the taxi accelerated down the road.

Within minutes Stephanie walked through the entrance foyer and took the lift to her floor. Outwardly she appeared composed. No small achievement, when inside she was a mess of conflicting emotions, uppermost of which was the need to hit out in restrained anger at Ghislaine's obsessive behavior.

'You have two urgent calls to return, three faxes are on your desk and your three o'clock appointment has rescheduled thirty minutes early.'

It was back to work with a vengeance, and she continued at a punishing pace until five. The worst of it had been dealt with, and what hadn't could wait until tomorrow, she decided wearily as she shut down the computer, collected her bag and exited the office.

Raoul was waiting for her in the downstairs foyer, and her heart skipped a beat at the sight of him. His dark suit was perfectly tailored, his grooming exemplary. He really was something else, she conceded as she drew close. She'd miss him like hell when he left.

'Hi.'

Her greeting was bright, too bright, Raoul decided as he took in her pale features, the air of fragility apparent.

'Tough day?' he queried lightly, and saw her faint grimace.

'An understatement.'

With a swiftness that surprised her he captured her mouth with his own and kissed her. Thoroughly.

She could only gaze at him in startled surprise when he lifted his head, and he smiled, watching her eyes darken and dilate. 'You looked as if you needed it.'

She did, but not for the reason he imagined.

Traffic was heavy, and it took twenty minutes to reach Mermaid Beach.

'I'll go shower and change,' Stephanie intimated as they entered the house. 'Help yourself to a drink.'

He let her go, and crossed into the kitchen, selected something nonalcoholic from the refrigerator, then entered the lounge.

The bank of framed photographs caught his attention, and he picked up one of Stephanie holding Emma as a young baby.

He traced her outline with his finger, his lips curving slightly at her celluloid smile, the brave tilt of her head. Strong, courageous, she possessed integrity, passion, and a sense of self he found admirable.

Emma's father had been a fool, he accorded silently. In more ways than one.

Raoul replaced the frame and crossed to the window, then stood looking out over the grass to the neat bordered garden running the length of the fence separating the house next door. Flowers bloomed in carefully tended clumps, and there were shrubs, a few palm trees indicative of the tropical Queensland climate.

Stephanie found him there as she entered the lounge, and he turned, taking in her slender frame, the light red-gold hair styled in a neat bob, the delicate facial bone structure.

'Stunning,' he complimented, noting the way the electric-blue silk emphasized her cream-textured skin and highlighted her eyes.

'Shall we leave?'

Raoul caught up his keys and followed her out to the car. 'You'll need to give me directions.'

'It's not far.'

The private home was owned by a wealthy client who was known for his generosity and his penchant for entertaining. Located in a one-way street running parallel to the foreshore, the extensive three-level mansion was one of many very exclusive homes overlooking the ocean.

There were perhaps thirty invited guests sipping champagne and indulging in bite-size canapés.

'The purpose of this soiree is business?' Raoul inclined as more guests drifted into the large lounge.

'Definitely. Charles is one of the firm's most influential clients.' Stephanie wrinkled her nose at him. 'Who likes to lead into the festive season with the first of the pre-Christmas cocktail parties.' A faintly wicked smile tugged the edge of her lips. 'Yes, I know. It's only the first week in November.'

During the ensuing hour they mixed and mingled, together and separately as Raoul was drawn into conversation while a guest snagged Stephanie's attention.

She was good at her job, he perceived. Her interest was genuine, and she had a head for dates and figures that earned her respect from her peers.

His gaze lingered as she laughed spontaneously at someone's joke, then moved easily into conversation.

At that precise moment she lifted her head and looked at him, aware instinctively that he'd been watching her, and she smiled, offering him a slightly raised eyebrow in silent query.

Was it possible for two people to communicate without words? Did he sense that she wanted him so badly she could almost feel his touch?

Stephanie felt the heat rise deep inside, sensed the prickle of awareness scud across the surface of her skin, as she endeavored to contain her wayward thoughts.

With a sense of fascination she watched as he murmured a few words to the man he was with, then he made his way toward her.

'Having fun?' she lightly teased as he drew close, and almost melted beneath the warmth of his smile.

'By any definition,' Raoul drawled, and lifting a hand he trailed the pads of his fingers across her cheek.

Her eyes flared, and she was willing to swear her lower lip shook a little in involuntary reaction. She felt her body sway fractionally toward his, almost as if it had a mind of its own.

'Hungry?' He let his hand trace the length of her arm to her wrist and threaded his fingers through hers. 'For food?' she countered with a wicked smile, and felt the faint pressure as his fingers curled around her own.

'That, too.'

'I know of an intimate restaurant not far from here that serves the most divine Italian food.' She waited a beat. 'We could take some home and have a feast.'

'You don't want candlelight, Chianti and Andrea Bocelli singing sweet ballads on the CD player?'

She felt a bubble of laughter rise in her throat. 'Well,' she conceded, offering him a deliciously seductive smile. 'If you insist on an authentic ambience.'

They left a short while later, and it took only minutes to reach the small restaurant situated in a long block of shops fronting the southbound highway.

Owned and operated by an extended Italian family, they were greeted at the door by a courtly uncle, served wine by the eldest son, a daughter served the food, while both parents and the uncle's wife reigned in the kitchen.

The aroma of fresh herbs and spices mingled with wine and a host of tantalizing sauces, and there was music…

'Pavarotti,' Raoul drawled as Stephanie opted for a table, 'Making me wait, hmm?' he murmured with a teasing smile as he followed her to a spare table on the far side of the room.

'It's called anticipation.'

'I'll get my revenge later.'

Her eyes gleamed with wicked humor as they each took a seat. 'I'm trembling.'

'As well you should.'

Raoul ordered a mild red Lambrusco, and they settled on a starter each and followed it with another, rather than a main, choosing a clear soup, followed by spinach and feta ravioli served with mushrooms.

'Perfecto,' Raoul declared when they finished the dish and ordered coffee.

It was after eleven when Raoul paid the bill and they left. The night was warm, and the sky held a myriad of stars, heralding another fine day tomorrow.

How many more days did she have left? Two, three? Don't think about it, a small voice cautioned. They had the night, and it was enough. It *had* to be enough.

Yet how could it be, she agonized hours later as she lay spent beside him. A long, slow loving so incredibly tender she'd almost wept as he brought her to orgasm, then just as she thought it was over he took her soaring to impossible heights and beyond.

Afterward she had pleasured him, embracing every muscle, annointing every inch of skin in a flagrant trail that left him groaning with a need so intense it was almost beyond control.

What followed was nothing less than a pagan coupling, primitive and unrestrained as they were driven by an intoxicating frenzy that was wild, erotic and totally shameless.

Slowly, with infinite care, Stephanie slid out from beneath the covers, caught up her robe and moved silently down to the lounge.

Moonlight slipped through the partly open shutters, and she adjusted them slightly to ensure a clear view of the yard. Everything was still, and the moon cast long shadows from the few trees and shrubs.

In the distance a dog barked, then quietened, and

she stood gazing out into the opalescent night, silent and lost in introspective thought.

It was there Raoul found her, after stirring and finding an empty space beside him, and he'd moved quickly, silently, through the house until he reached the lounge and saw her slender form outlined beside the window.

Something tugged at his heart. She stood so still, so obviously lost in thought. How long had she been there?

Her arms were crossed at her midriff, and she looked so alone, almost forlorn.

'Unable to sleep, *cherie?*' he queried quietly as he moved to stand behind her. He slid his hands around her waist and drew her back to rest against him.

Stephanie felt his lips caress the delicate pulse beat at the edge of her neck, and let herself sink into him.

'It's a beautiful night,' she said huskily, and felt a sensation arrow through her body as he nuzzled an earlobe.

'*Oui.*' His fingers splayed down over her stomach and slid between the opening of her robe. 'I have to fly back to Paris at the end of the week.'

Her heart lurched, then stopped beating for a few seconds. Pain seeped through every pore in her body, and she could almost swear she forgot to breathe.

The moment she'd been dreading had finally arrived. Why, in her wildest dreams, had she hoped that it wouldn't?

What could she say? *Don't go?*

'I want you with me.'

Paris? *Paris.* It wasn't possible. How could she even consider it? What about Emma? Celeste was wonderful, but she couldn't expect her mother... Besides, there was her job. 'We live different lives on opposite sides of the world.' She was breaking up inside. 'But we don't—'

'Have a future?' His hands slid to her shoulders and he turned her around to face him. 'Yes, we do.'

Pride was responsible for the way her chin lifted, and her gaze was steady. 'As sometime lovers who spend a week or two together whenever the timing is right?'

'No. I have something different in mind.'

'I'm not *mistress* material,' she assured sadly.

His teeth showed white as his mouth curved to form a musing smile. 'I'm relieved to hear it.'

'I have a child, a career,' she stated.

'This career, *here,* is too important for you to give up?' Raoul queried.

'I have responsibilities, financial commitments.'

'If the financial commitments were removed?'

'What are you suggesting?'

'Marry me.'

Shock deprived her of the ability to speak, and when she found her voice, the words emerged as little more than a whisper. 'What did you say?'

'Marry me,' Raoul repeated gently.

'You're not serious?'

'I can assure you I have never been more serious in my life.'

'But—'

'If a career is so important to you, I can arrange a position in marketing, or any field you choose.'

She didn't doubt it. 'Raoul—'

'I have an apartment in Auteuil, and a home in the Chinon wine region of the Loire Valley. Emma will delight in spending weekends and holidays there.'

'You're going too fast,' she protested.

'No,' he denied quietly. 'I want you with me, as my wife, wherever I happen to be in the world. Emma is a part of you that is everything to me. Perhaps in a few years there will be a sister or brother for her to love and care for. But for now, we share whatever the future holds...together.'

Stephanie felt the prick of tears, and fought hard to control them.

'I have important meetings in Paris next week. Four days, *mon amour,* then I'll be back and we will arrange our wedding. Your parents will return to Paris with us for Christmas.'

Christmas was only weeks away. 'It's too soon...we can't—'

'We can. Easily.' Money, sufficient amounts of it, had a power of its own.

'You love me.'

It was a statement, not a query. She could only wonder at her own transparency, and how long he'd known.

He cradled her face in his hands, glimpsed the fleeting emotions, and appraised each and every one of them. 'I took one look at you that first day on the film set,' he revealed softly. 'And knew my life would never be the same again.'

Any minute soon she'd wake and discover this was nothing more than wishful thinking on the part of her subconscious mind.

'Be with me, stay with me. Eternity. *Je t'aime, mon coeur.*'

Her bones turned to liquid, and she wound her arms around his neck and pulled his mouth down to hers, initiating a kiss that reached to the very depths of her soul.

'I fought against becoming emotionally involved with you every step of the way,' Stephanie revealed in a voice just above a whisper. 'I tried so hard to convince myself you were a complication I couldn't afford. But everywhere I turned, there you were. I couldn't seem to escape you.'

His lips were creating an evocative path at her temple, and she could almost feel his smile.

'You noticed.'

'You didn't play fair. You charmed my daughter, not to mention my mother.'

'They were my strongest allies.'

'It was almost as if you had a hidden agenda.'

'Assignment,' Raoul corrected, and nuzzled her soft curve at the edge of her neck. 'Father to Emma. And husband…*yours.*'

It took her a moment to catch her breath, then a slow sweet smile curved her lips. 'Reverse the order,' she teased unmercifully. 'And I might think about it.'

'Might you, indeed?' Raoul growled huskily. He swept an arm beneath her knees and lifted her against his chest.

A bubble of laughter escaped her lips. 'What is this, persuasion?'

'Sweet torture,' Raoul assured huskily. 'Until you say *yes.*'

It didn't take long. Not very long at all.

CHAPTER ELEVEN

THEY were married by a Celebrant in a civil ceremony held in a restored nondenominational church set in beautiful gardens by the river. Stephanie's father gave her away, Celeste was matron of honor, and Emma the flower girl.

The bride wore a short cream dress overlayed with scalloped lace, while the groom was resplendent in a perfectly tailored black suit.

Afterward they ate fine food and drank Cristal champagne.

Two days later Raoul, Stephanie and Emma, together with Celeste and Philip flew to Paris where they held another ceremony, a reaffirmation of their vows, for the benefit of Raoul's family.

Sandrine and Michel attended, as did Anneke and Sebastian. Henri stood proudly as head of the family, and Madeleine, the elderly matriarch, gave her blessing and thanked Stephanie for introducing a great-grandchild into the family. Premature, perhaps, for the legal adoption that would change Emma's surname from Sommers to Lanier would not be official for a while.

Two Lanier wives hid a secretive smile, and remained silent. It was too soon to share the news that next Christmas, God willing, there would be two babes for Madeleine to fuss over.

Raoul noted Stephanie's faintly wistful expression and linked her fingers with his own.

'Happy?'

She turned her head toward him, and her radiant smile took his breath away.

'Yes,' she said simply, amazed that he needed to ask, when every night she responded to his lovemaking with such a wealth of unbridled passion. 'How would you feel about—'

'*Oui.*'

'I didn't finish.'

He lifted her hand to his lips and brushed a lingering openmouthed kiss to the pulsing veins at her wrist. '*Mon coeur,* you don't need to.'

Her eyes sparkled with wicked humor. 'You read minds?'

'Yours, *mon amour,* is particularly transparent.'

'That's something I'm going to have to work on,' she said with mocking amusement, and heard his soft husky laughter.

'You are the other half of me, part of my soul. I look at you, and know your mind, your heart, as well as I know my own.'

'*Tu es ma vie. Je t'adore.*'

His mouth brushed her temple. '*Merci, mon ange,*' he said gently, and felt her fingers tighten around his own.

Life, he acknowledged, didn't get any better than this.

HARLEQUIN®
SUPERROMANCE®

You are now entering

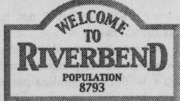

WELCOME TO RIVERBEND
POPULATION 8793

Riverbend...the kind of place where everyone knows
your name—and your business. Riverbend...home of
the River Rats—a group of small-town sons and
daughters who've been friends since high school.

The Rats are all grown up now. Living their lives and
learning that some days are good and some days
aren't—and that you can get through anything
as long as you have your friends.

Starting in July 2000, Harlequin Superromance brings
you Riverbend—six books about the River Rats and
the Midwest town they live in.

BIRTHRIGHT by Judith Arnold (July 2000)
THAT SUMMER THING by Pamela Bauer (August 2000)
HOMECOMING by Laura Abbot (September 2000)
LAST-MINUTE MARRIAGE by Marisa Carroll (October 2000)
A CHRISTMAS LEGACY by Kathryn Shay (November 2000)

Available wherever Harlequin books are sold.

HARLEQUIN®
Makes any time special ™

Visit us at www.eHarlequin.com   HSRIVER

If you enjoyed what you just read,
then we've got an offer you can't resist!

Take 2 bestselling love stories FREE!

Plus get a FREE surprise gift!

Coming Next Month

HARLEQUIN *Presents*

THE BEST HAS JUST GOTTEN BETTER!

#2121 THE ITALIAN'S REVENGE Michelle Reid
Vito Giordani had never forgiven Catherine for leaving, and now, seizing the advantage, he demanded that she return to Naples with him—as his wife. Their son would have his parents back together—and Vito would finally have…revenge!

#2122 THE PLEASURE KING'S BRIDE Emma Darcy
Fleeing from a dangerous situation, Christabel Valdez can't afford to fall in love. But she can't resist one night of passion with Jared King. And will one night be enough…?

#2123 HIS SECRETARY BRIDE
Kim Lawrence and Cathy Williams
(2-in-1 anthology)
From boardroom…to bedroom. What should you do if your boss is a gorgeous, sexy man and you simply can't resist him? Find out in these two lively, emotional short stories by talented rising stars Kim Lawrence and Cathy Williams.

#2124 OUTBACK MISTRESS Lindsay Armstrong
Ben had an accident on Olivia's property and had briefly lost his memory. Olivia couldn't deny the chemistry between them— but two vital discoveries turned her against him….

#2125 THE UNMARRIED FATHER Kathryn Ross
Melissa had agreed to pose as Mac's partner to help him secure a business contract. But after spending time with him and his adorable baby daughter, Melissa wished their deception could turn into reality….

#2126 RHYS'S REDEMPTION Anne McAllister
Rhys Wolfe would never risk his heart again. He cared about Mariah, but they were simply good friends. Their one night of passion had been a mistake. Only, now Mariah was pregnant— and Rhys had just nine months to learn to trust in love again.

CNM0700